BULL

BRAWLERS

J.M. DABNEY

CONTENTS

1 TO FIGHT OR TO FUCK, DEFINITELY, FIGHT

The sun began to crest above the tree line as Archer "Bulletproof" Woods squeezed his hand around the water bottle he wished was an ice-cold beer or a glass of bourbon. The plastic crinkled and threatened to collapse in his big hand. It was ten years, two months and thirteen days since his last drink. Most days he got through it without thinking about it, but moments like tonight it clawed at his gut and was a rage he barely suppressed.

Every night at work he ended his shift by staring into a double of his favorite bourbon. Reminding himself of why he was sober. Repeating the count and adding a new day, yet tonight he'd almost taken that drink. Imagined savoring the smoky burn as aged liquor flowed over his tongue and down his throat. Bull would let it warm all the places that were cold inside him—the dead places.

At eighteen he'd done what was expected of him. He'd married his high school sweetheart. Polly, a beautiful blonde with a figure most men would've drooled over, but not him. Bull had loved her like a friend, even after all these years they were still friends. It wasn't long after the wedding he'd enlisted in the Marines. He had hoped it would have saved them from a miserable life together. That was nineteen-seventy-nine, he'd hopped a bus to boot camp and left a pregnant, frightened wife behind.

He'd served his country for twenty years before he'd retired and followed in his father's footsteps as a blacksmith. Bull had been an asshole for most of his life. Muscular and macho, his sexuality above reproach. All the while he'd made him and his family suffer.

Forty-three years he'd lived in the closet, drank away his pain and denied to everyone including himself what he actually wanted. After over two decades of marriage, he'd asked for a divorce and drunkenly confessed to Polly he was gay. She'd accepted it quicker than he'd thought. They'd both lived in the hell of his making. Even if he couldn't be happy, he wanted Polly and their son Hank to have a chance.

It had been thirteen years since he'd made the confession. The first couple of years he had stumbled his way along, one hookup after another, and it wasn't what he'd expected. His coming out should have brought him a sense of freedom, but that's not what he got.

He had been an alcoholic in his early forties; Bull was passed his prime and only trying to move on.

Over a decade later, Bull consisted of harsh, rough edges. A face that told his journey in deep lines and faded scars. He wasn't pretty or soft, neither was he handsome. Bull was just homely and old at fifty-six. Security in a gay biker bar, nothing especially noteworthy. He played father to a group of men who lived in his house who were just as damaged as him.

The warmth of the sunrise touched his face, and he squinted his eyes. Bull should go inside and get some sleep, yet he didn't want to crawl into his empty bed only to await his nightmares which never stopped raging inside him. Taunted by his regrets and where he thought he should be.

With a deep exhale, he pushed up from the rocking chair, turned to jerk open the screen door and walked inside. He made a detour in the kitchen to toss his water bottle in the recycle bin. The beautiful Twitch ran the house like his own. Twitch was a bartender at Brawlers and was married to the Head of Security, Crave. Their bosses, Scary and Tank stepped down to spend more time with their husband.

He headed for his bedroom on the second floor and once he was in his room he kicked the door shut behind him. Bull pushed his unbuttoned jeans off his hips and down his legs, then kicked them off. He crawled into his unmade bed and laid down, crossed his arms under his head.

His home turned into a Brawlers' Crew halfway house. For a decade, he'd given the crew with no family or place of their own a home. He wouldn't admit it, but he liked having other people in the house. It wasn't so quiet. It was the distraction he needed.

Hunter was the newest member of the crew. He hadn't quite figured out that boy yet. The man could fuck up breathing.

Psycho who lived up to his name most of the time moved into the cottage on the other side of the fence with his boyfriend a few months before, along with Bernie, Psycho's ex-wife, and Bernie's wife. They'd decided to co-parent a brood of potential kids. Stacey found out a few months ago she was pregnant. Shocked the fuck out of them all. They'd tried once. Apparently, Psycho wasn't shooting dust like Bernie accused.

To be honest, how the fuck Crave and Psycho found men baffled him. Bull had gotten to the point he couldn't even find a fuck for the night. Although a few months of abstinence had turned into two years without more than his left hand to get off. He'd come out to have more than that, but it hadn't worked out as he'd thought. His sobriety hadn't given him the opportunity to find a man of his own.

He yawned wide until his jaw popped and flipped over onto his stomach. Bull wrapped his arms around his pillow and tucked it under his head. Hopefully, he was tired enough the nightmares wouldn't come. He felt himself slowly drift to sleep.

■■■■

"There better be coffee left," Bull grumbled as he shuffled into the kitchen at a little before one.

It sounded like Crave, Twitch, and Hunter were up for lunch. Psycho's voice also joined in. Psycho's boyfriend would be at his bakery at that time. Bernie and Stacey worked during the day.

"I made a fresh pot." Twitch held out Bull's huge mug. "I heard you coming."

"Thanks," Bull muttered and turned to lean back against the counter. "What's with the house meeting?"

"Landon and Zerk's anniversary party is tonight. We'll have some new faces, but most of the guest list was familiar names." Twitched answered from his position on Crave's lap.

"Shit, the fresh meat gets the fuckers all worked up." Bull hated working the party nights. Mainly it was only the

Twirled Crew who brought in strangers. Mostly their guests were laid back—didn't cause shit.

"Let's cut capacity in half, keep out the hardcore fighters."

"I'll need Psycho inside with me." Bull sipped at his strong coffee.

"Got no problem with that. Crave can take care of the shit at the door. Ben's coming tonight. I won't have anyone else watching my boy."

Psycho was obsessive about Ben's safety. Ben didn't seem to mind one fucking bit. Psycho grew up in a community who fought for hierarchy, the weakest were tortured and used on a daily basis. No one fucked with Psycho's boy.

"We'll figure out more of a plan when we get to work. Right now, Twitch needs some attention." Crave smirked as he stood and tossed Twitch over his shoulder.

"Gag him this time, his screams could fucking break glass," Hunter complained but never looked up from his coffee or laptop.

Crave loudly laughed as he took off at a run. Bull shook his head.

Hunter arrived at his farm with no past or work experience, the man didn't try to share or hang out all that much. His secretive nature grated on Bull's nerves. Bull could sense trouble, and Hunter screamed it loud and clear.

"I'm going to go shower." He turned and topped off his coffee, then headed back to his room. Psycho and Hunter quiet behind him, at least those two knew how to not fill the silence with useless conversation.

He groaned at the sound of what had to be Crave's hand connecting with Twitch's ass and then the infamous squeal. He just hoped like fuck his shower drowned it out.

He set his mug on his dresser and stripped out of his pajama bottoms. Maybe he should move into Psycho's trailer behind the barn for some peace and quiet.

Dammit, they were going to drive him from his own damn house. He stepped into the shower, turned on the water and as he feared it didn't drown out the grunts and screams or the sound of a headboard banging against the wall. He was kicking Crave's ass for that later—that was fucking guaranteed.

2 WHAT THE HELL WAS HE THINKING?

What the hell was he thinking, it was Gregory Charles's only thought as he walked into Brawlers Bar and instantly stuck out. Where he'd worn a pinstriped designer button-down shirt and dark slacks he was surrounded by leather and denim. He nervously raised his hands and smoothed his perfectly styled hair which was longer on top and shorter on the sides. His uncontrollable waves tamed with too much product.

He looked around trying to spot Landon. His employee and friend invited him to his fourth-anniversary party. He'd thought it would be fun, but now he wasn't so sure.

"Gregory," Landon's voice drew his attention.

Gregory snorted and smiled at the crazy man standing on the bar waving his arms. He noticed Zerk, Landon's husband reaching up to pull Landon from the bar, but he was laughing too hard to get a hold on him. Those two men were crazy.

He wove through the crowd as he kept his gaze on Landon. Gregory started to trip as he felt a hand on his ass and he spun to confront the offender, but all he could see was the center of a wide cotton covered back. Powerful muscles strained against the shirt.

"Hey, don't touch," a dangerous, gravelly voice made him back up a step. "We don't touch someone else property, do we fucking understand each other?"

He didn't catch an answer, but the huge man who'd stepped in to protect him turned. Gregory tipped his head all the way back. A gorgeous man with a scowl stared down at him.

"You must be Landon's boss, I'm Psycho, I'll escort you to the bar."

His tongue wouldn't work, and his mind was completely blank. He was sure he should say something, but nothing was coming out.

"You're cute, and all, and the awe is stroking the ego, but—"

"Psycho," A soft voice came from his right, and he turned to find a graying man, deep laugh lines beside his twinkling blue eyes.

"Yes, Ben," Psycho asked as his massively muscled arm reached out and tugged the older man to his side.

"Don't try that innocent stuff with me. Quit embarrassing the newbie."

"Yes, dear," Psycho ruined the innocent tone with a snort.

"It's a wonder I love you."

"Don't be mean, Ben."

Gregory stared at them with his mouth hanging open. The large dangerous man gently tipped Ben's chin up with his fingertips and brushed a soft kiss on the man's mouth. Psycho gave Ben a look so loving it almost made Gregory sigh.

"Hi, I'm Ben." Ben held out his hand as he was tucked under Psycho's arm.

"Gregory, it's nice to meet you."

"Don't let Psycho give you a hard time, he's really good at it. Come on." Ben stepped away from Psycho.

Gregory instantly found himself being tugged forward by Ben through the crowd—a crowd which couldn't separate fast enough.

"My boyfriend is highly protective. He's threatened everyone that if they touch me, they're dead. He won't do it, well, maybe he won't—"

Gregory laughed nervously. This is not what he'd expected when he decided to spend an evening with Landon. He was ready to go home.

"Don't even think about it," Landon whispered in his ear.

"What was I thinking?"

"About escaping, not happening. I see you've met Ben and Psycho."

"Someone grabbed my ass, Psycho stepped in."

"He's not as bad as he looks. Elijah completely loves him. I'm so glad you came. Come on let me introduce you to everyone. You'll never remember everyone's name, and besides, there are too many weird ones."

Gregory found himself in the middle of a group of men and women. He was bombarded by names, drawn into conversations he regretted instantly. A blond with dreadlocks was the worst of them. He had no filter.

He sipped at the beer he hadn't wanted until hours passed and he realized he was enjoying himself. Everyone was friendly and open. Yes, they didn't know what polite conversation was, but it was refreshing to not always be on alert—to always be picture perfect.

He checked the time to find it close to 1 a.m., and Landon's group appeared to be the only ones left.

"I'm going to the bar to get some coffee, do they have—"

"With Elijah here, they've got a pot going all the time."

"Okay, I'll be right back."

Gregory slipped from the booth and strode to the bar, a man he was introduced to earlier named Twitch was wiping down the glossy surface. He slowed as he noticed the neon and overhead lights shimmered off liberally silver streaked black hair. It was shaggy on top and combed back, buzzed on the sides. The man was staring down at a glass of amber liquor. Big hands wrapped tightly around the glass. He seemed to be having an internal debate, one second he was lifting it to his mouth and the next slamming it down with barely suppressed anger.

The anger is what made him hesitate. Arnold, his husband of five years, was an angry drunk. He'd already had Psycho come to his rescue, so maybe the man wouldn't mind doing it a second time.

With a fortifying breath, he continued and took a seat beside the man. Wow, the strong profile hinted at a rugged face.

"What can I get ya?" Twitched bounced up.

"Coffee, black."

"Elijah's favorite." Twitch reached down and produced a mug, flipping it over to set it in front of him.

"Make it two." Gregory didn't know what made him say that and nodded toward the man beside him.

"Whatever the handsome man wants." Twitch quickly produced another mug and filled both. "Just holler if ya need anything else."

"You're only supposed to flirt with me, Twitch."

A blond behemoth he faintly remembered maybe named Crave and married to Twitch leaned on the bar.

"How do you think I make my tips?"

"Oh, you're so in for punishment when we get home."

Gregory was about to defend the man when a broad smile broke out on Twitch's beautiful face.

"And? Maybe I like—"

Gregory blocked out their conversation and focused on his coffee. The man beside him hadn't taken his eyes off the rock glass. He seemed to be inhaling the scent of whiskey or whatever through his nose and then through his mouth as if tasting the aroma. The stranger didn't seem to be paying any attention to Gregory's existence at all.

He curved his fingers around the mug and absorbed the warmth through the ceramic. It was weird, and he didn't know why the man fascinated him. Gregory could admit he was attractive in a rough, bad boy sort of way, but maybe the man was too old to be considered a bad boy. His silver beard was in need of a trim.

"Did anyone ever tell you, Boy, it's not polite to stare?"

Holy shit, the voice was a sexy rumble with an edge of growl.

"Boy? I haven't been a boy in a long time."

The snort he received wasn't friendly. "What are you thirty?"

"Thirty-six, thank you."

"You're two years younger than my son, definitely a boy."

"Someone is running for Grumpiest Old Man of the Year Award." Gregory turned his attention back to his coffee and raised the mug to his mouth. He savored the strong brew as he regretted sitting beside the man.

"Play nice, Bull," Landon's voice came from behind him, and Landon threw his arms around Bull's waist.

"When have you known me to be nice, Landon?"

"That's true. Ten years and you're still an asshole. At least you're consistent."

"You're asking to have your ass reddened?"

"That's the plan when Zerk gets me home."

Bull's rough chuckle took Gregory by surprise. A hairy arm lifted and reached back to ruffle Landon's hair. He'd didn't think he'd ever seen that much hair in his life. Arnold waxed everything every couple of months to the point his body hair came in light and fine.

"Go on, you freaky little shit, I ain't got time for you." Bull teased Landon's waves one more time before bringing his arm back down.

"You always have time for me, besides you haven't introduced yourself to my boss yet. Gregory, this is Bull, Bull, this is Gregory, be nice and say hello, Bull."

Glittering eyes, one blue and one green turned on him, they were beautifully clear, crystallized shades, oddly pale. "Gregory."

"Nice to meet you, Bull." He didn't bother extending his hand because he knew the man wouldn't take it anyway.

He observed as Bull pushed his glass away and picked up the mug.

"I better get going. I didn't tell Arnold I'd be out so late."

"I'm sure it'll be fine. He's out of town anyway."

Yes, anyone else it would probably be okay, but Arnold got mad if—Gregory pushed away the thoughts. There wasn't much he did that made Arnold happy. When Arnold got home, he was going to give Arnold the divorce papers.

"I'm sure, but it's late, and I'm normally in bed long before now."

"You early to bed, early to rise people make me sick."

He chuckled at Landon's disgusted tone, then looked up to find Bull watching him. Bull's eyes were empty of emotion, but it felt as if that gaze was burning through him. As if all his secrets were exposed to Bull. He jerked his stare to Landon and forced a smile.

"I know, a total party disappointment."

"I'll walk you out," Bull announced.

"I'm sure—"

"You're sure of a lot of things, but I'm still walking you out."

Landon gave him a quick hug, and he slipped off the stool. "How much for the coffee?"

"I got it covered," Bull's tone didn't allow for refusal.

His first moment of real fear hit him. Years of practice helped him hide it, he shoved his hands in his pockets to disguise their shaking. A soft, growl had him darting his eyes to Bull and knew he was caught.

"Let's go."

Gregory walked beside Bull to the exit. The parking lot was deserted, and there were spotlights at the corners of the building facing the lot. With the neon Brawlers sign off, he could only make out the outline of his black car.

"Next time park closer to the building, employees and their partners have all the spots at the front. Take one."

"I don't know if I'll be coming back. This isn't—"

"Not your scene, yeah, kinda figured that."

"I didn't mean to offend you."

Rough fingers grabbed his upper arm, "You didn't. Get in."

Gregory got in his car as quickly as he could and started his car. Bull stayed beside the spot until Gregory was pulling out. He could still feel the strength and warmth of Bull's grip around his arm. He shook his head as he focused on the road ahead. There really wasn't a reason for him to rush home. The thirty-minute drive turned into an hour one before he pulled up in front of his house in one of the richer neighborhoods.

He hadn't liked it, but Arnold picked it out since he was paying for it. Gregory lifted his hand and pushed the remote for the garage door. His heart sunk to his stomach and he turned nauseous as he saw Arnold's car in his usual spot.

He almost put his car in reverse and pulled out, but knew his punishment would only be worse if he delayed it. The abuse, mental and physical, became something he was used to, and he knew he shouldn't have. That wasn't the way a marriage was supposed to be, hell, it wasn't how it was at the beginning. Two years ago, he'd earned his first insult, shortly after that, his first slap.

Gregory shook his head, turned off his car and exited it, then made his way into the house through the kitchen door. The bright light came on as soon as he closed it behind him.

"I saw you tonight, how many of them did you fuck before you came home," Arnold asked in a slurred voice.

He didn't have a chance to defend himself before the back of Arnold's hand met his cheek, and he was at the mercy of his drunk husband.

3 BULL'S GOING TO JAIL

The insistent ringing of his phone drew his attention away from his furnace as he worked on a custom bed frame for an old client. He could still feel the heat through his protective clothing. That ringing though was getting on his last nerve. He threw down the wrought iron bar with the half-done curve, pushed his welder's mask up, and strode to his workbench. His jerked his gloves off and picked up his phone.

Bull answered without checking to see who it was, "What?"

"Aren't you a ray of sunshine this lovely morning?"

Landon's voice made him roll his eyes skyward and hope for patience. He hadn't slept last night, so he was a little short on his temper. It's why he was spending the morning in his workshop instead of sleeping. He didn't want to think about why he hadn't closed his eyes, and it didn't have anything to do with craving a drink, although he wanted to drink his new problem away.

"What do you want, Landon?"

"I need your help."

"You okay?"

"I'm fine, but I'm not so sure about my boss. You remember him from the other night?"

He remembered him, smooth, tanned skin, long, lashed green eyes and a lean body that—*married man*, Bull, he yelled at himself.

"Yeah, the pretty boy, stuck out with his designer gear."

"He called out sick the whole week, I've gone to his house a few times, but no answer. One night Arnold came to the door and told me Gregory wasn't there. I'm getting worried, Arnold isn't the nicest man and he creeps me out."

There was what was driving him the craziest, a single microsecond of fear and Bull knew. Men fought each other, it happens, and there wasn't anything wrong with it, but a man doesn't put his hands on his partner—no matter woman or man.

"What do you want from me?"

"I called the cops to do a wellness check, but nothing came of it, either they didn't go, or they took Arnold's word for him being okay. Go with me to the house, I need to see Gregory make sure he's okay."

"Why me?"

"Because you're six-three and over two hundred pounds of intimidating man. One of your thighs is bigger around than my waist."

"Exaggeration, Landon."

"Not really, I've studied them, you have great—"

"Off track and you're distracting me, so I'll go along with whatever fucked up plan you've got in your head. So just spit it out."

"If something did happen to Gregory, he's gonna need a place to stay for awhile…a safe place surrounded by huge manly men."

Gregory in his house, no, he couldn't fucking do it.

"Please, I know you're thinking of ways to say no, but just come to his house with me."

"I can do that, where do I meet you?"

"I'm waiting outside."

"Confident?"

"When have you been able to say no to one of us?"

Landon, Twitch, Elijah and Brody, along with Bull's nieces Juvie and Princess didn't get told no often or at all. He was weak when they batted their lashes and gave him a sweet smile. Bull was a pushover for those six.

"Dammit, fine, but you're gonna get me as is." He disconnected the call and strode out of his workshop pulling his old threadbare t-shirt off to wipe down his face, chest and under his arms.

"Here, Bull," Twitch called out as he ran up to him.

Twitch held out a t-shirt, his wallet, and keys, and his other hand to take his dirty shirt.

"You in on this too?"

Twitch just smiled and said, "Go get your boy." The man skipped away.

"He's not my boy," Bull roared.

"Shouldn't call his name when you get off then." Twitch turned his look over his slim shoulder.

"You know I fucking didn't." He paused as he took in Twitch's too sweet expression. "Have your stuff packed by the time I get back."

"Yeah right," Twitch yelled and let the screen door slam behind him.

Bull pulled on the t-shirt as he headed for Landon's car. Landon was laughing his fool head off, and Bull growled as he opened the passenger door.

"Can't you buy a bigger damn car?"

"Shut up, Giant, just because you're cranky and shit."

He hit the switch to roll down the window as he tried to shove himself into the toy car. No sooner did he have the door closed, Landon was backing up. He quickly pulled the seatbelt around him and buckled it to Landon's amusement. Bull turned to stare out at the scenery speeding by.

Bull was leery about what he'd find when they got to Gregory's house. He'd fought most of his life, and he had countless scars to prove it. The thought the younger man even had one bruise on him pissed him off. Bull wanted someone of his own, but he sure as shit wouldn't admit that to anyone.

The man's husband thinking—he shook off the thoughts because it wasn't a foregone conclusion, maybe Gregory was actually sick. Landon could just be acting like a drama queen.

A half hour later they pulled into one of the nicest neighborhoods in Powers. The houses were all cookie cutter, suburban perfection. Some Rockwellian utopia with perfect little white picket fences and manicured lawns. It made his skin crawl.

They slowed to a stop in front of a house that could only be described as a showpiece. He didn't know Gregory, but he really couldn't see him living in a place like that.

"Now, don't do anything rash, I just want—"

"I know what you want, but I'm not going to promise anything. If his husband put his hands on him, the bastard needs to be punished."

"Fine."

Landon didn't say anything else, and they got out of the car, he followed close behind the smaller man. Bull's usual scowl in place and as they stopped on the porch landing he crossed his arms over his chest.

Landon raised his hand to push the doorbell. It wasn't long before they heard muffled steps on the other side. When the door opened, Bull felt himself snarl. The man framed in the doorway was about his height but muscled like a runner or swimmer, not a brawler. Even on a Saturday morning, the man wore a dress shirt and expensive slacks with high polished dress shoes.

"Landon, I already—"

The guy's voice was smooth and cultured, each syllable enunciated to hide any sign of an accent.

"I don't give a shit what you told me, I want to see him."

Bull noticed the man's fingers curled into his palms. He moved his larger body between Landon and Arnold. A muscle ticked in the man's jaw. It was the only sign other than the fists that betrayed Arnold's anger.

"Motherfucker, I wouldn't think about it," he warned. "Now, you're going to let Landon inside to check on Gregory. If he's fine, we'll be on our way, if not, you better call the cops now."

Bull stepped up as Landon darted around him and Arnold and into the house calling Gregory's name. Arnold tried to grab Landon, but Bull caught his wrist.

"We don't touch without permission."

Arnold tried to shake off Bull's grip, but Bull was a hell of a lot stronger. He crowded the thinner man back against the door. Even at ten a.m., he could already smell the alcohol on the other man's breath.

Is that what Gregory liked? Slick and handsome. Bull was an asshole, but he wasn't a bastard, and that's exactly what Gregory's husband was.

"You're making a mistake, I'll—"

"You won't do shit, man, I've got more than fifty pounds on ya, and I fight for a living. You throw a punch, and I'll make sure you don't get back up."

"I'm calling the co—"

"Call them you, bastard," Landon's enraged voice had him turning to find him leading Gregory down the steps.

Every step Gregory took appeared to cause him pain. There were bruises, but they'd faded until they gave Gregory's complexion a jaundiced appearance. He even looked thinner than he had a week ago. His plump lips were dry and cracked.

"He fell down the steps, no big deal."

The words were barely out of the fucker's mouth before Bull wrapped his hand around his throat.

"I know you ain't that fucking stupid," Bull growled and then turned to glance at Landon, "Did you pack him a bag?"

"No, I just—"

"Get him to the car and come back, pack whatever he needs. Gregory, tell Landon what you need." They passed behind him talking quietly, and it sounded as if Gregory was giving Landon a list.

He didn't take his attention away from Arnold. Bull wanted to teach the bastard a lesson, but there'd be time enough later. Right now, he was getting Gregory back to the farm. He'd have a security detail organized by the afternoon.

"You can't take him—"

"Oh, but I can, and I'm going too. From this point on, he's mine, and don't fuck with what I own."

Landon stepped up beside him out of his blind spot. "I'll be about five minutes, he has a go-bag hidden away."

Bull nodded. The fact Gregory had a hidden bag enraged him more. This shit wasn't a recent occurrence, but how long had Gregory put up with this shit?

"You're going to regret this, I'll ruin—"

"Ruin what, asshole, you might run the game where you come from, but you ain't got shit to do with my world. Also, if you think you're gonna fuck with my crew, we'll bury you, got it?"

Arnold didn't have a chance to answer before Landon appeared with a large duffel bag and laptop case.

"Is that all he wants?"

"Yeah, except this," Landon held out a Manila envelope. "It's the divorce papers."

Bull took it and slammed it against Arnold's chest. "Sign them."

"I'm not letting him go."

"We'll see. Go on, Landon, start the car."

He stepped back as Landon exited the house. That's when he saw it, the shifting of Arnold's shoulder, and instantly raised his arm to block Arnold's punch. He countered and struck with his left. Arnold's head connected with the door as he slid down it to sit on the polished hardwood.

"When you throw a punch, don't lead with your shoulder. It lets your opponent anticipate your move. You're a bad ass when you're taking on someone who can't defend themselves. Don't make that mistake with me."

Bull left the man sitting there. "Sign those fucking papers, I don't want to have to come back." He threw the statement over his shoulder as he strode to the car.

Gregory was curled up on the backseat. A blanket was wrapped tightly around him, and his eyes were closed. He ignored the urge to slip into the backseat and gather the man into his arms. Instead, he forced himself back into the front seat. Landon pulled away from the curb and headed back toward the farm. Once he had Gregory on his turf, he'd figure out what the fuck he was going to do with the fragile man. His life definitely wasn't one designed for Gregory, but Gregory would have to get used to it—at least for now.

4 RETRIBUTION WAS COMING, GREGORY JUST DIDN'T KNOW WHEN

Cool, refreshing water flowed over his tongue, and he tried to gulp it down. Gregory was so damn hungry and thirsty. He hadn't been allowed out of his room in days. Maybe Arnold wasn't mad at him anymore.

"Easy, honey," a gruff voice soothingly rumbled.

His eyes flew open, and it all came rushing back. Landon rushing into his room. Bull and Arnold facing off. His whole body jerked as he tried to get away.

"Calm down, you're safe," that was Landon.

Gregory turned his head to find Landon watching him with a concerned expression. He was so—Landon saw how he lived. The walk-in closet he lived in. His bare mattress on the floor. Tears stung his eyes as he pulled away and rolled to the opposite side of the bed.

"He's going to punish me for this, you have to—"

"Get that thought out of your head now. You're staying right the fuck here. No arguments."

Bull's voice broached no argument, and big hands forced him onto his back. Bull loomed over him. Their faces inches apart. He swallowed hard as he pulled his arms to his chest and placed his hands on Bull's thick, rounded pectorals. Bull's skin was hot through the thin cotton of his t-shirt, and there was a cushion of hair beneath it. A hand with thick rough calluses cupped one of his cheeks.

"This is your room. Landon already unpacked and put your stuff away. Twitch made you some soup. When I get back, you'll eat and get some more sleep."

Bull surged from the bed and disappeared out the open door.

"I made him mad."

"No, you didn't make him mad. Arnold did that."

"Why did you even come to the house?"

"Are you insane? I don't see you for a damn week, no call, no nothing, then when I got to your house no one answers." Landon sat on the edge of the bed. "The one time I do get one, Arnold tells me you're not even home. What choice did I have, but to get Bull?"

"Why him?"

"Have you seen him, two hundred and fifty pounds of brutal street fighter? I could've gotten Psycho, but Ben would kill me if his man went to jail. Twitch would probably like a break…well Twitch's ass anyway."

Gregory's face felt like it went up in flames.

"You're so easy."

Gregory sighed, "What am I going to do? I can't—"

"Bull says you can stay here as long as you want or at least until you get Arnold to sign the papers."

"He doesn't have—"

"We gave them to Arnold and Bull strongly suggested he sign them."

"Why did you two do that?"

That was going to make everything much more difficult. Arnold loved to dole out punishment. It hadn't always been that way. His husband hadn't ever been loving, but Arnold cared about him.

"Because you're my friend and Bull can't say no when you smile sweetly and bat your lashes, remember that?"

Why did he have to remember that?

"What happened to you, Gregory? Why didn't you ever tell me?"

"It wasn't always like that. Arnold got a new job. More business meetings and dinner, he always drank—"

"Don't make excuses for him. He had you locked in a closet."

"He only locks me in when...I shouldn't have gone to Brawlers."

"Make one more fucking excuse, and you'll regret it."

Gregory jerked his gaze to the door to find Bull's large body filling it. His shoulders almost touching each side.

"Bull," Landon yelled.

"What, he's staying here, he's getting a divorce. It's the way it's going to be, but right now he's going to eat."

Bull approached the bed with a tray of food. Whatever he was giving him smelled amazing. He hadn't eaten since Arnold locked him in. Gregory was only allowed out to use the bathroom. He hadn't even been allowed a shower and only cleaned up quickly in the short time he'd had outside his room.

"Twitch thought you should start with something light. Chicken and rice. Twitch makes the best bread. Scoot up," Bull ordered.

The man had a tendency to order him around, and he shouldn't obey, but he did. He set up, Landon fluffed the pillows behind his back, and as he settled into them, Bull placed the tray over his lap. Bull straightened to stare down at him. The lines deepening between his thick brows.

"Don't eat too fast and sip your tea. I've gotta get ready for work. Landon said he'd hang out with you. Me and the crew will be home sometime after 2 a.m. so don't panic if you hear us moving around. You'll hear the motorcycles coming anyway.

"Make yourself at home. Landon will give you tour after you eat."

"Thank you," Gregory whispered as he stared down at his tray. His stomach growled, and his bottom lip quivered.

"Eat. If you go outside, stay out of my workshop. Oh, Twitch's rat escaped. If you find Pinkie, see if you can get him back in his cage. I swear that beast knows when they're going to lock him up."

"How can you lose a rat with a hot pink color?"

The conversations these people had were weird and confusing. Rats named Pinkie. Bull being nice—to him anyway. The innuendo in the bar the night of Landon's anniversary party.

"I don't know, but he did, and if I find it in my bed one more time, I'm putting it in the barn. How the hell did he talk me into getting a pet?"

"Um, same way me, Elijah and Brody, and your nieces get away with everything. You adore us to distraction."

"My nieces definitely, not so much the rest of you."

Landon laughed loudly as Bull flipped Landon off before kissing Landon's cheek and walking out of the room.

"The man who gets him will have his hands full," Landon said in a stage whisper. "In more ways than one."

"Fuck you, Landon," Bull hollered from somewhere down the hall.

"Is that an offer?"

Bull growled loud enough to be heard down the hall. Landon only snickered and rearranged the bowls and platters on Gregory's tray.

"You better eat some before Bull comes back to say goodnight."

He didn't ask why Bull would come to say goodnight. He just focused on his food and ate slowly, it didn't take him long to start feeling full. Everything was so good though. The soup wasn't overly seasoned and was perfect for his stomach, the bread was light, and he couldn't remember the last time he had homemade bread. He just nibbled absently on the bread and sipped his tea as Landon curled up in a chair beside the bed. The man just watched him, and he was about to ask him to stop when Bull appeared again.

The clean scent of body wash and deodorant hit him first then he was transfixed on the broad, sturdy chest covered in a thick mat of silver streaked black hair. It continued to taper down his firm stomach to the low-slung jeans. His large muscled frame was sexy.

Even all that silver hair covering the bulging muscles. A man old enough to be his father shouldn't look—he wasn't going there. He'd just left his husband. He was living in a stranger's house for however long it took him to get his life on track. Gregory was confused, and it was screwing with his head.

"Close your mouth," Landon whispered in his ear.

"Shut up."

That only made Landon chuckle.

"I'm out. Behave while I'm gone," Bull ordered

"But, Daddy, can't I have a boy over."

"Never call me Daddy again."

"You know you like it."

"You're a pain in the ass, Landon."

"But you love me."

"Begrudgingly, yes."

"You're always so sweet to me…Daddy."

Bull shuddered and once again disappeared, but faster than earlier.

"If I wasn't hopelessly in love with Zerk, I'd jump that man in a heartbeat."

Gregory didn't like that. He also didn't like his friend calling Bull Daddy. He hurt, and he was tired, and it was all too much.

"Are you done?"

"Yes, thank you."

Landon stood, approached the bed and picked up the tray.

"Why don't you lay down and try to get a little more rest, when you get up I'll show you around. Maybe we can have a little search party for Pinkie."

"Okay."

Gregory just wanted to be left alone so he could think. He turned over and pulled the covers up to his chin. When his lawyer drew up the divorce papers, he hadn't really thought about when he'd give them to Arnold. He'd planned to do it several times the past month. Each time he'd chickened out. Arnold never went as far as he had since Gregory came home from Brawlers. He'd always avoid Gregory's face, but that's where he'd focused the last beating.

He squeezed his eyes shut as tears started to fall. He was safe—for now, but it was only a matter of time until Arnold came for him. Gregory curled into himself hoping for sleep and a clearer head when he awoke.

5 BULL KNEW THIS WAS A MISTAKE

Another night of no sleep and watching the sunrise tortured him, Bull kicked the rocker back and forth. He was getting too old for this shit. Gregory was asleep in the room next to his, and he swore every time the man rolled over in bed he heard it. Three days and the temptation was torture. He'd make himself take a nap soon. The screen door creaked, and he turned his head, he almost groaned as Gregory stood holding the door open.

"Don't you sleep," Gregory asked.

"Until recently, yeah."

"If I'm too much—"

"It's got nothing to do with you," Bull lied, but it was partially true. Just because he couldn't get his brain to realize he couldn't have the man it wasn't Gregory's fault.

"May I join you then?"

"Sure, can't sleep?"

Gregory sighed as he eased the screen door closed and walked around him to take the seat on the rocker next to his. Gregory had a throw blanket tightly wrapped around him.

"All I've done is sleep for days. I'm not used to having so much free time."

"I gave you the password so you could work from home."

"I know, thank you. And I wanted you to know I appreciate you for letting me stay here. I'll find a place as soon as I can."

"Don't worry about it. We have an open-door policy around here. Crave needed a place to crash when he first started working at Brawlers that was almost ten years ago."

"I heard you've had a lot of people staying here. You seem like a man who likes his privacy."

"Having other people here kind of fills the quiet. Some days I wish it was quieter than it is."

"Oh, thank you for the earplugs, are they always that loud?"

Bull snorted and turned to find Gregory giving him a horrified look. Crave and Twitch were notoriously noisy. He was waiting for Gregory to run back to town the moment he caught them on the back porch, barn, or wherever else the mood struck them.

"They've been behaving since you've been here."

Bull couldn't help laughing loud as Gregory's eyes widened and his jaw fell. To be honest, Twitch and Crave were ten times worse before Gregory moved in. They'd even taken to turning their music up to try to dampen the volume.

"That's behaving, I'd hate to hear them—"

"Keep the earplugs handy."

"It must be nice though."

The wistfulness in Gregory's voice confused him.

"What?"

"Being wanted that much."

"Do you mind me asking you something?"

"Sure."

He turned his attention back to the sunrise and gathered his thoughts. Bull wondered how he could ask without sounding like he was judging.

"Why did you ever get with Arnold?"

"Well, we were both career oriented. I was getting my Legal Research Firm's reputation built up to the point I could scout the best. Arnold worked long hours in Atlanta for his law firm. His goal was to make Partner. We could spend a whole week apart. Neither of us was particularly clingy."

"Is that what you wanted or what you settled for?"

"You definitely don't pull punches."

"Not in my nature, so answer."

"Bossy. The short answer, it's what I settled for. Long answer, I never saw myself having a long-term relationship. I hook up with a lot of cheaters or ones that don't treat me…shit, I've never been with someone like Arnold. He was driven and dedicated. It definitely wasn't all romance. When he asked me to marry him, there were doubts, but I said yes anyway.

"The moment he realized he wasn't making partner at his old firm, he found another job, and everything changed. He was so angry all the time."

"And he started taking it out on you?" Bull forced his hands not to curl into fists.

"At first he just became hypercritical of everything about me. He didn't want to introduce me to the people he worked with, and I think he was hiding…several nights he came home without his ring on. His drinking became a huge issue, and I believe he was using drugs, but couldn't prove it."

"When did he start putting his hands on you?"

"Do we—"

"Yes, answer," Bull ordered.

"It started out with a slap when I asked him was he cheating because he stopped wearing his ring. I don't know why I didn't leave. I wanted too."

"You had a go-bag."

"I hid the bag in the attic. It was just cash and a week's worth of clothes, all my important papers. I keep suits at the office for dinner meetings. One day I came home, and he accused me of looking at another man. Swore he smelled someone else's cologne and he took me upstairs to our bedroom, locked me in the closet after knocking me around. I'd seen him mad, but he was enraged, he only let me out to go to work. Made me call him every hour to check in with where I was and with whom. That was a year ago, and I packed the bag."

"You know you don't have to worry about that shit anymore, right?"

"He's going to try to get me back and pun—"

"Not happening. He has no power here. Besides his shit works in the corporate arena, but he doesn't want to fuck with the Brawlers or Twirled Crews."

"I don't want to cause you all any trouble."

"All we have is trouble. A little more won't hurt anything."

"Why do you stare into a glass of whiskey?"

"Turnabout and all that shit, huh?"

"Yeah."

"I got married at eighteen because being gay wasn't normal. Marrying a woman and having kids, providing for your family. I married Polly the day after I graduated high school and two months later I joined the Marines."

"Must have been hard on her."

"It…we'd just found out she was pregnant."

"I remember you said you had a son older than me."

"He just turned thirty-eight. He's divorced. Career military. Just started dating this great woman. He said she's a widow. Her husband was killed in Afghanistan. She has two young kids."

"Possibly a grandpa."

Bull groaned and dropped his head back, he rolled his head to look at Gregory. "I didn't need another reason to feel old."

"Men don't get old, they get distinguished."

Bull snorted at Gregory's impish expression.

"Baby, I'm old." He almost cursed at the endearment, but Gregory didn't seem to pay attention to it.

"Don't think I didn't notice you're trying to distract me from the whiskey."

"Fine, now who's bossy. I drank away my misery, to numb the pain of hiding who I was. I loved and do love Polly as a friend, and I made her life harder than it had to be. Years passed, and my drinking got worse, it wasn't just drinking after work to unwind before going home. It turned into a shot of whiskey to start my day, a flask to get me through the day. I drunkenly confessed one night I was gay."

Fuck, he still remembered that night in a haze. There wasn't any surprise on Polly's beautiful face just a look of resignation.

"How'd Polly take it?"

"A lot better than I thought she would. She's a helluva woman. Had to be to put up with my ass for twenty-five years. We divorced thirteen years ago. Newly single at forty-three and trying to figure out how to be gay, for three years it was drunken tricks in bathrooms, alleys, bathhouses, cheap motels. I couldn't take it anymore. I came out to be free and—"

"And you felt more trapped."

He didn't know how he felt about Gregory zeroing in on his predicament. Telling the younger man about his past was easy and hard at the same time. He laid out all the ugly parts and his failures.

"Yeah, so ten years ago I walked into my first AA meeting. Every night I sit down, stare into a double of my favorite whiskey, remind myself why I'm sober and repeat the count. Then I place it on the rail and walk away. Just to prove to myself I'm stronger."

"The other night though it looked like you were going to drink it."

Bull hadn't thought anyone noticed. The crew always let it go as one of his quirks like all of them had. A stranger at the time noticing, well, not just a stranger but Gregory seeing him at his weak point.

"I almost did. Most days I get through without even thinking about it and others I'm just so damn thirsty. Does it bother you to be in the house with an alcoholic with a temper?"

"It should, but you've been nothing but nice. Okay, you're kinda a grumpy bastard, but at your advanced age what else did I expect."

"You got jokes, great just what I needed in my house another smart ass."

Gregory laughed, it was husky, and it moved over Bull like a caress. The man's full, wide smile was beautiful and lit up his already gorgeous face. Before he realized what he was doing, he was running the backs of his fingers down Gregory's cheek.

"You should do that more often...the smile looks good on you."

"Th...thank you."

Bull brought his arm back to rest on the arm of his chair before he did something stupid like tracing those kissable lips. One taste of the man and he knew he'd have Gregory in his bed. Once there, Bull wouldn't let Gregory leave it until he thoroughly fucked his sexy, rounded ass. He'd own every inch—Bull cut off that line of thought before it got his mind anymore fucked up.

"I better get to bed."

"Yeah, I'm still a little tired."

"Come on then." Bull pushed himself from the chair and held out his hand.

Gregory hesitated for a moment before taking it, and Bull pulled him up. The man stumbled for a second and Bull steadied him with his hands gripping Gregory's slim waist. His thumbs pressed into the slightest softness. Bull wanted to savor it. He hadn't had a lot of soft things in his life. His life and job were hard, nights of barely leashed violence and his own undercurrent of rage.

"After you," Bull said as he released Gregory.

Gregory didn't run, but he hurried into the house. Bull almost chuckled as Gregory caught the screen door right before it slammed behind him.

Bull could swear he could still smell hints of soap and laundry detergent, mixed with a slight lingering of a scent that was all Gregory. He closed his eyes as he ran his thumbs along the calloused pads of his fingertips and then fisted his hands. The compulsion to follow Gregory slammed into his gut. The man was only separated from his asshole ex for a matter of days, but Bull still wanted to claim that beautiful body until the man couldn't remember a time when Bull wasn't touching him—fucking him.

He swallowed hard and took deep calming breaths until he felt it was safe to enter his house. Sleep, that's what he needed. Everything would seem better, and he'd be more himself when he awoke.

6 THERE WAS SOMETHING SEXY ABOUT STRONG, ROUGH HANDS

"You're not supposed to be here." Gregory stared across the desk at Arnold who stood in the doorway of his office.

The man was impeccably dressed, every hair in place, and almost too handsome. Arnold's perfection put him on edge. He'd spent five years of his life with the man and looking at him at that moment he didn't understand what he had seen in him.

"This stupidity of yours needs to end. I've put up with it long enough. I'll forgive your little fling. We all make mistakes."

He stepped back to put another layer of protection between them. The desk and the chair weren't sufficient, but it's all he had. Then what Arnold said registered.

"I'm not having a fling. I'm staying with a friend of Landon's, nothing more."

"You can't be that stupid. You fucked him, no man is that possessive without getting a taste."

Bull was nice, maybe a little too hardened by life, but Bull had treated him great since he'd moved in. The man didn't treat him any different than he did Twitch or Landon.

"I didn't sleep with Bull. He's been very—"

Arnold's fists clenched at his sides.

He flinched and walked backward until his back hit the wall. He hated himself for the reaction. Fear was an emotion he'd rarely experienced until the last few years. He knew just what the flat of Arnold's hand felt like connecting with his cheek. Memorized the texture of Arnold's closed fist to his midsection. The weight of Arnold's slender, muscular body holding him down as Arnold punished him for one offense or another. Most of the time, he hadn't even known what he'd done.

"Has he been nice, Gregory? Men aren't nice without strings attached. You're coming home."

"I'm not. This hasn't..." He cleared his throat to rid it of the knot of fear that threatened to choke him. "This hasn't worked in a long time. I want a divorce. We're not..." He closed his eyes but quickly opened them when he heard to soft fall of footsteps.

Arnold advanced, and he tried to make himself as small as possible. He anticipated the pain he would experience.

"Mr. Charles, you have a meeting."

His secretary, Martha, announced loudly as she walked into his office. He'd give her a raise, a huge raise.

"Thank you, Martha."

"This isn't over, Gregory, you will come home. You don't have a choice."

Arnold whispered, but from the hardening of Martha's features, he knew she had heard. The man angrily turned and stormed from the office. Martha barely made it out of Arnold's way.

"Are you okay, sir?"

"Yes, yes, I'm fine. Thank you, Martha."

He was grateful she hadn't asked any more questions, and she turned from the office. This wasn't going to end quickly. Arnold wasn't going to let him go, and he couldn't stay with Bull at the farm forever. As soon as he'd left, his protection would disappear, and he'd once again be at the mercy of his husband as he had been before.

He checked the time and decided to head home, no, not home, just the farm. It was easy enough to work from the kitchen table or the living room couch. He quickly gathered up the files he'd need for a few days.

■■■■

Gregory was so tired by the time he reached the farm, he parked Bull's truck beside the man's motorcycle and cut the engine. A week away from the office and he was out of practice. He transitioned to a Brawlers' schedule too easily, and now 6 a.m. was torture. The confrontation with Arnold hadn't helped. It seemed to take all the energy he had left.

Gregory tiptoed out of the house that morning so as not to wake anyone. Two pots of coffee and he could've still taken an afternoon nap.

"Don't you look all fancy," Bull's voice came from behind him, and he turned.

All thoughts of Arnold disappeared at the view in front of him.

His mouth almost fell open but gritted his teeth. Sweat made the thick hair on Bull's chest shimmer under the early evening sun. Jeans hung low on slim hips showing off the top tight pubic curls. That deep V probably framed a beautiful package to perfection—oh shit, he was in trouble.

"Is thirty-six too old to find a new career?"

"And why is that?"

"Because 6 a.m. sucks."

"We turning you into a night owl," Bull asked.

Bull stepped farther away from the building he used as a workshop. His large hands were covered in black. He remembered Bull stroking his cheek, and there was something sexy about strong, rough hands. Gregory never thought about that much. He'd always dated men with soft hands, the corporate night-to-five type. Bull was the exact opposite.

"I got used to sleeping until the afternoon."

"Didn't take you long to get lazy."

Bull stopped a few steps from him, and he inhaled the tang of sweat and a hint of Bull's soap. He almost leaned forward to pull Bull's scent into his lungs.

"I'm not lazy. You not working tonight?"

"No work this evening. I spent all afternoon in my shop. Got an appointment at Twirled in an hour, want to come along? Maybe we can corrupt you with some ink."

"No, I'm quite happy without putting myself through the self-inflicted pain."

"Sometimes pain is a good thing in the right situation."

"I'll take you word for it."

"So, want to come along, and maybe you'll change your mind about the virgin skin."

"I just need to change."

"I gotta jump in the shower first. We'll take the bike. I have an old helmet you can use."

"I've never ridden before."

"All you have to remember is to move with me and enjoy the ride. Now, come on, get out of the suit. It looks weird on ya."

"I'll have you know this is a perfectly tailored suit. Functional yet classic style."

"Whatever you say, baby, let's go. Zerk gets cranky when I delay him going home to Landon's ass."

"Y'all are way too open about sex talk."

"And you're wound way too tight," Bull said as he threw his arm over Gregory's shoulders and steered him toward the house.

"I'll have you know that I'm very fun."

"Yeah, yeah, whatever you say, baby."

Gregory nearly stumbled as Bull nudged him forward and grabbed his shoulders. Strong hands kneaded his tensed muscles, and Gregory groaned.

"Oh, that's nice."

Bull's thumbs massaged the back of his neck, and Gregory let his head fall forward. The pads of Bull's fingers were thick with callouses and teased his skin just right.

"You're tense as fuck."

Bull's voice was rough as he spoke near Gregory's ear. His cock twitched, and he squeezed his eyes closed, thinking unsexy thoughts. It wasn't working especially when Bull stroked the front of his throat. There was a slight pressure, but it eased, and then Bull pulled back.

He almost begged Bull to continue. That would be an appalling idea. He was married—no he was separated. He took the four steps to the landing and reached for the screen door, but Bull reached around him and pulled it open.

"You got twenty minutes, pretty boy."

"Asshole."

"Now you're cussing, wow, next step tattoo."

"Not happening," Gregory threw over his shoulder as he headed for his room to get ready.

He needed to find a place of his own and soon before he did something he'd regret. Gregory was more worried about not regretting something happening between him and Bull. Why was he even thinking about it? Bull was just being nice because of Gregory's situation and him being friends with one of Bull's best friends. He saw things that weren't there. He closed himself in his room and hurried to get changed so he'd be ready when Bull finished.

Four hours later, he was curled up on one end of an over-stuffed couch and his face hurt from laughing. Gregory covered his mouth as he nearly spewed water all over the coffee table as Lucky danced out of Bull's reach.

"Not my fault you're old, shame a man your age with your significant endow—"

"I will let Crave kill you next time you mouth off if you don't stop talking about my dick."

"Dude, you're hung like—"

Gregory couldn't help it when he snorted. The conversation was entirely inappropriate and uncomfortable since it centered around Bull's package, but Lucky's impish expression as he took advantage of Bull being stuck in the chair.

"Don't you start too, baby, I got enough shit dealing with them."

"Come on, it's a blind date, your left needs a break. Have you seen the size of your forearm lately?"

"I hate you."

"No, you love me, but I'm already taken."

"Priest is a fucking saint. I would've left your crazy ass by now."

"He's smarter than you."

"Gregory wants ink, all virgin skin."

Gregory's eyes widened at Bull's evil expression as the hyper Hippie turned on him. That lean, muscled body stalked across the room, and Gregory suddenly felt like prey.

"No, I said no."

"But, but, Gregory," Lucky whined as he leaped over the coffee table and landed on the couch beside him in a crouch.

"No, but, it's not happening."

"If not a tattoo, what about a piercing. Are your nipples sensitive?"

"What," Gregory squeaked.

"If they are, imagine your man tugging on them with his teeth as he—"

Gregory slapped his hands over Lucky's mouth. He didn't want to think about sex. He didn't want to think about Bull, but if sex entered his brain, that's who would star in his fantasies. Gregory was already having enough of those.

Bull liked being shirtless way too much.

Lucky swatted his hands away, and his lips widened in a smile bordering on maniacal. "Maybe a Guiche, it's a piercing through your perineum. Your partner plays with it during oral or sex, placed right, and it stimulates—"

"No, Lucky," Gregory said as he put his hands on his hot cheeks.

"Your boy's a prude, Bull." Lucky pouted and stepped off the couch.

"I'm not his boy."

Lucky mumbled something which sounded suspiciously like not yet and returned to his station just as the door opened. The chime drawing everyone's attention. Gregory was off the couch and across the room before the door swung closed behind Arnold. The man looked completely out of place among the flash art on the walls and photos of the artist's work. He moved as close to Bull as he could get. Zerk even shifted to the side as Bull reached out to wrap his hand around the back of Gregory's thigh.

He knew Arnold leaving earlier was too easy.

"Dropping off those papers," Bull asked in a quiet voice with a lethal edge.

He was thankful that Bull took over because he couldn't speak if his life depended on it.

"No, I came to pick my husband up."

Bull rubbed soothing circles on the back of his thigh, and Gregory leaned closer.

"Actually, you're separated, and Gregory and I have plans. So, unless you signed the divorce papers, there's no reason for you to be here."

Even with the anger, he felt radiating off Bull, his touch remained gentle.

Gregory kept darting glances at Arnold and couldn't get his tongue to work. He was frozen in fear. He hadn't fully recognized that he was actually happy at Bull's place. Nothing was expected of him, and he didn't have to worry about a hit coming at any moment. Even when the guys fought, which was a lot, he never felt afraid.

"Gregory—"

"I think you forget what I told you, I own every inch of him. You don't fuck with what's mine."

Gregory noticed the hum of the tattoo machine hadn't ceased or slowed down. Although, Lucky and Zerk seemed to be on alert. It was in the way they held themselves, and Lucky watched Arnold. He didn't doubt if the man made one move toward him, Arnold wouldn't get near him.

"My husband knows where he belongs, his place."

"Yeah, my bed, now—"

Bull stopped as Priest walked in with Juvie and Princess, with a baby sling strapped to his chest. Matty, his one-year-old son, secured to Priest.

Priest seemed to instinctively know something was up and ushered the girls quickly through the shop. "Gregory, come with me." Priest grabbed his hand and dragged him toward a door marked Employees Only.

He thankfully left the battle building in the other room. Arnold's pupils were blown, and if he wasn't mistaken, Arnold was high on something. He wasn't going back. Finally, he was happy and safe, and he wouldn't give that up for anything.

"Juice box?" Princess skipped to the fridge and pulled out a box for each of them.

Juvie curled up in a huge moon chair and pulled out her sketchpad. She wore an expression very much like Scary's. For not being blood-related the teenager was very much like the big man.

"Trouble's picking them up in an hour. They had a day off for some teacher in-service day."

A bright mop of ginger hair caught his attention, and he tamped down the urge to ask to hold him.

"Want to hold him?"

"Are you sure?"

"Of course." Priest smiled sweetly and lifted the baby from the sling.

The cutest fat cheeks and two-toothed smile almost made him make the unmanliest squeal as he took the baby. He'd never wanted kids of his own, but he loved kids, they were all so nonjudgmental. He held Matty carefully against his chest. Lucky and Priest used a surrogate, he'd heard Lucky's sister offered to carry for them.

"Matty is used to being handled all the time. Lucky barely lays him down, along with the rest of the Twirled and Brawlers Crews."

"He's gonna be spoiled."

"I think he's already there. The crews have spoiled Princess and Juvie rotten, so Matty's getting the same treatment."

"Matty being charming," Bull's voice had him turning to the door.

"I think he's trying to lure your man away."

"Don't you start too. You've been married to Lucky way too long," Bull said as he walked up to Priest and leaned down to kiss his cheek.

"A lifetime couldn't be long enough."

Gregory watched Priest's face as the man said it and every word was true. It was one of the things he'd learned quickly about the Twirled Crew, Crave and Twitch and also with Psycho and Ben their devotion to their partners was unquestionable. It was there in every look and touch, existed in every smile a few whispered words caused. Again, he was envious. He was in his late thirties, and he'd never come close to anything like that.

"How's my boy," Bull asked as he leaned over Matty.

Bull's thick finger stroked Matty's cheek, and the man's thick wavy hair tickled Gregory's cheek.

"Am I still watching him when you and the crazy Trenton's go away for that festival," Bull asked he straightened and turned toward Priest.

"You sure you still want to do it?"

"I already took the that Friday and Saturday off."

"We really appreciate it."

"Just because you're parents now, you still need some time just the two of you."

"I think Lucky's going to be a bigger wreck than I am."

"You two will be fine. Besides Gregory will be there to help do all the diapers."

"I think not, I never agreed to that."

"We'll see, you ready to go get dinner or do you want to go home?"

"Can we just get take-out? I'm not particularly in the mood to be social."

"Whatever you want."

Bull gently took Matty and held him up as he blew raspberries on the fat tummy exposed by the tiny, scrunched t-shirt.

"Don't get him worked up. It's almost nap—"

Priest groaned as Matty giggled and fisted his little hands in Bull's hair.

They were so cute together. The big grumpy man baby talking and tickling the chubby baby was a striking contrast.

"Give him to me, you're as bad as Lucky," Priest scolded as he plucked Matty from Bull's hold.

"Hey, don't be mean." Bull turned toward him, "What do you want for dinner?"

He wasn't really hungry, he wanted to know what happened after he left the room. They said goodbye to everyone and headed for the front door with Bull holding his hand the entire way. Gregory knew it was for show, but a big part of him wished the man would touch him for real.

Gregory had bigger problems though. What had Arnold done or said? His transition to a new life wasn't going to be easy, but he sure hoped it didn't turn out to be hell.

7 BABYSITTING 101

Oh shit, he'd forgotten kids hated sleeping all night. Bull fed and changed Matty. Now he laid in bed with Matty's small, chunky body sprawled on his bare chest with a stuffed rat tucked under his arm. Of course, Lucky and Priest wouldn't get their kid normal stuffed animals.

He'd be miserable tomorrow. Since Gregory moved in, he hadn't been sleeping enough as it was, throw a baby on top of it, and he snapped at everyone. He yawned, and his jaw popped. Bull was a light sleeper. He could nap, but if Matty even made a sound Bull would be awake.

"Exhausted yet," Gregory's amused whisper came from his open door.

"It's been thirty-eight years since I did this and Polly got Hank through most of this stage." He still remembered the letters he got while he was away from home training or on missions. Hank didn't like sleeping. He was picky about his food. He also got the funny stories of what Hank was up to. Bull needed to get in contact, but Hank wasn't due home for leave until next month.

Gregory chuckled softly and walked quietly into his room. The younger man curled up on the left side of his bed with his head on Bull's pillow. That was probably not a good idea, but he didn't open his mouth to say anything. Gregory reached out and stroked Matty's hair.

"I didn't think this through when I offered to babysit. They're doing Attachment Parenting and co-sleeping."

"Is that what the three-sided crib is for?"

"Yep, but apparently Lucky and Priest snuggle Matty a lot because he's not having anything to do with his bed."

"Maybe it's because it's a strange environment."

"Yeah, and they said if he cries at night he's not allowed to self-soothe he's to be snuggled."

"Matty's going to be spoiled."

"Attachment parenting and radical honesty, they're going to spend a lot of time in the principal's office."

"Sounds about right." Gregory rolled to his stomach and hugged the pillow.

"Shouldn't you be sleeping. Don't you got some meeting in the morning?"

He'd moved Gregory in almost a month ago. Arnold was still making a nuisance of himself, but he didn't know if it had gotten worse or better. He had a feeling Gregory wasn't telling him everything. That evening Arnold showed at up Twirled, he'd made it clear for the man to stay away. He wasn't listening, and Bull was losing his patience, which was already short due to extreme frustration.

"Landon's handling it. I just called him so I can watch Matty and you can sleep."

"Baby, I've run on less sleep and been just fine." The endearment came naturally, and he'd ceased trying to stop it weeks ago.

"Yeah, but, Grump, you're like a rabid bear, snapping at anyone who steps wrong. The harmony of the house depends on your sleep."

"Smart ass." Without thinking he reached out a smacked Gregory's ass. "Shit, sorry."

"It's okay."

But something in Gregory's tone said it wasn't.

"I shouldn't have done that."

"It's fine, Bull," Gregory said as he scooted closer and pressed his forehead to Bull's bicep. "I'm not as fragile as everyone thinks."

"I fucking know that."

"Watch your language, Matty's first word—"

"You've met his dad, right?"

"Okay, that was stupid."

Gregory's soft laugh eased Bull somewhat but didn't quell his urge to sooth the cheek he'd spanked or the fact he wanted to do it again—harder. He wasn't going there. The need to kiss and touch Gregory grew stronger every day, and it wasn't just some passing thing. He was fucking falling for the man, and that would be a mistake. What would the younger, handsome man want with his old, surly ass?

The man treated him like the rest of the guys did, well, how Twitch, Landon, and Brody did. He didn't notice even an ounce of attraction on Gregory's part. Matty jerked in his sleep, and he slowly rubbed Matty's small back until the baby relaxed.

"You're good at that."

"Babies have basic needs, eating, sleeping, diaper changes and comfort and safety. I'm just glad I'm the Uncle now. I can spoil him and give him back."

"Aw, didn't want more than the one?"

"Polly couldn't have any more after Hank. There were complications." He leaned his head to the side until he rested his cheek against Gregory's soft hair.

"I'm sorry."

"Polly's husband is younger than her. He had three young kids when they got together, and she got to spoil more kids."

"Was it weird when—"

Gregory lifted his head, and Bull noticed the single furrow between his brows that signaled he was thinking or analyzing. He was so careful about what he said and how he said it. Gregory seemed happier and more relaxed lately, but Bull still noticed him occasionally watching himself.

"No, it's one of the reasons we got divorced as quickly as we did. I wanted her to have a chance at a healthy relationship."

"What about you?"

"Since I've been sober I wanted…" He stopped trying to figure out what to say and how to explain. Gregory seemed to be moving closer because he was pressed fully to Bull's side and his head on his arm. Bull shifted until he could slip his arm under Gregory. He hoped it didn't end badly with him making a fucking fool of himself.

"Wanted what?"

"I needed to be fine alone, and it sorta turned into a habit. When you're in your mid-forties and early fifties you're pretty much stuck in your ways."

"But you've tried to date?"

"Yeah, but men my age aren't exactly getting pounced on."

"Especially grumpy bears."

"You're fucking obsessed with my grumpy nature."

"It's actually pretty cute in a weird sort of way."

"Not cute, supposed to be sexy and distinguished, middle-aged bad boy."

Just then Matty lifted his head and rubbed his face against Bull's chest. He made little snuffling sounds that he was sure left baby snot in his chest hair.

"Nope, definitely cute."

"I'm getting ready to kick you out of bed." He must've growled a little too loud because Matty began to whimper. Gregory took a turn and rubbed Matty's back and then over his soft hair. He was shocked they hadn't woken him yet, but he'd heard Lucky and Priest stayed up late to have conversations while Matty slept beside them.

"Don't, this mattress is fucking amazing."

"Wow, was that an f-bomb falling from those virgin lips?"

"Ha ha."

"Definitely corrupted at Brawlers Farm."

"I like being here, you know that, right?"

"You're welcome to stay. As long as you don't mind communal housing and hearing people have sex all the time."

"It's not that bad. You can't deny that Crave and Twitch love each other. I've never seen couples like the Twirled and Brawlers ones before. They always know where the other is and touch for no other reason to assure themselves the other's there. The amount of affection even outside the couples amazes me. For a bunch of rough, hardened bikers, y'all are pretty damn affectionate."

"I think it's because not all of us had that and the ones that did it's something in their nature. It took awhile for me to be comfortable with it."

"You seem pretty good at it though."

"You're going to be as tired as I am if you don't sleep. We'll both be useless."

"Is that your way of telling me to shut up?"

"Would I do that?"

"No, no you wouldn't. I should go back to bed."

"Stay, you're taking over when you wake up anyway. If we fall asleep, you're in charge of his next cry."

"Deal."

He almost groaned as Gregory wiggled around until he got under the covers and resumed his spot with his head on Bull's shoulder. Gregory curved his arm around Matty.

"Goodnight, Bull," Gregory whispered as he settled in.

"Night." Bull closed his eyes knowing he wouldn't go to sleep right away but wanting to savor this one moment. Okay, it wasn't exactly how he wanted to get Gregory in his bed, but it was something.

Gregory would always have a place there just like any of the guys, but his decision was his hardest since he'd never had one moment of attraction to any of the others. Except it was more and that scared the fuck out of him. Bull was everything Gregory didn't need, and maybe he'd fucking remember that one day, just not tonight.

Bull turned his head and found Gregory asleep. He brushed a kiss on the man's forehead and tensed as the man whispered his name and snuggled closer to him and Matty. It was going to be a long ass night.

8 A KNIGHT AT BRAWLERS

He felt like he was on display, like some exotic animal, and it made him slightly uncomfortable. Gregory was also exhausted. How a baby only a year old could wear him out, he didn't know. He was definitely getting old. Bull couldn't be faring much better, every noise Matty made, and Bull woke up to reach for Matty.

Really for Bull's gruff nature and almost continuous scowl the man was sweet as hell. Gregory wouldn't tell him that though.

He sipped his coffee that caused an argument between him and Bull. Bull was insistent if Gregory wanted an actual drink he could have one. Gregory was never much of a drinker. Maybe a glass of wine at a business dinner, besides if he drank tonight he'd be asleep on the bar stool well before last call.

"Warm that up for you?" Twitch bounced over.

He adored the small man. Gregory never met someone that happy all the time. There wasn't anything Twitch wouldn't do for someone he cared about.

"Please." Gregory pushed his mug forward.

"The baby kicked your ass."

"Completely."

"That nephew of mine is adorable."

"That I can't deny." Gregory smiled then lifted his mug to his mouth. "He's like a mini version of Priest."

"Well, Lucky got what he wanted. He swore he was getting a ginger out of Priest." Twitched turned his head when someone called his name and then back at him. "You need anything just yell."

"Thanks."

Gregory was shocked at how his life had changed in less than a month. Until he'd come to live with the Brawlers, he hadn't realized how miserable he was. He'd known he was unhappy, but—

"Hi, can I buy you a drink?"

Whiskey scented breath fanned his face, and he eased back to find a man about his age standing way too close. He wasn't a bad looking guy dressed in jeans and a t-shirt that molded to a muscular upper body. At one time the stranger may have been someone he'd have a drink with, but not anymore.

"No, thanks." Gregory turned back to his coffee hoping that was that.

"Aw, come on, one drink, I'm Neal."

A soft fingertip ran along the wedding band he still wore, more out of habit than anything.

"Maybe come back to my place."

The sudden smirk on the man's face made him snarl his nose.

"Your old man will never know."

Gregory started looking around, not for help, but to get the guy to go away. He could call Twitch over, just as he thought it he caught sight of Bull. He smiled as he noticed the tightness of Bull's jaw and the low simmering anger in his gaze.

"Um, I'm not so sure about that." Gregory pointed over the man's shoulder.

Neal glanced back over his shoulder, and Gregory swore the man's face went ashen.

"Bull, hey, man, how you doing?"

"Is there a problem here?"

Man, when Bull's voice went gruff like that Gregory's mind went places it shouldn't. What the hell was it about the much older man he found so—irresistible? It went beyond the fact the man was gorgeous no matter what his age.

"I swear I didn't know he was yours."

"Is that right, and what the fuck you try to pull, Neal?"

"Not a damn thing."

"He tried to get me to go home with him. Swore you'd never know." He supplied an answer earning himself a glare from Bull and a terrified look from Neal. He did have to admit the angrier Bull became, the sexier he was, so he was likely playing with fire here.

"He's lying, Bull, I didn't even know—"

"If I were you, I'd be moving away from him and quick."

Neal couldn't get away fast enough and nearly tripped over his own feet in his haste to escape.

"Do you get that reaction a lot," he asked with a chuckle.

"You weren't helping."

He found himself trapped between Bull's body and the bar, with Bull's arms pinning him in with his hands on the glossy surface behind him. Bull had a tendency to do that; crowd him but not in a threatening way. To be honest, it was strangely comforting.

"True."

Bull snorted, "You gotta stop hanging out with the Twirled Crew, you've developed bad habits."

"I've spent more time with the Brawlers Crew than the Twirled one."

"We'll pretend you didn't say that. You look tired."

"We're never having kids," he said it loud enough to draw stares.

Bull lowered and shook his head. "I'm too old for them anyway."

"What were you saying in the wee hours of the morning?" Gregory pretended to think about it, "Oh yeah, something about sexy and distinguished."

Gregory reached out and caught the sides of Bull's t-shirt. Bull lifted his head, and Gregory studied the different shades of Bull's eyes. He loved the contrast.

"You're feeling exceptionally cheeky tonight."

"I'm delirious with exhaustion."

"But you're smiling, so it ain't all bad. If I get back to work, you going to behave yourself?"

"Probably not, but since everyone paying attention thinks I'm yours, I think I'll be left alone."

"They better. And no trying to go home with anyone else."

Two weeks ago those words would've sent him into a panic, but this was Bull. He liked it a little too much. He was probably losing his mind. His husband, no, soon-to-be ex-husband turned into an insanely jealous man, but Bull's possessiveness was sexy. Definitely losing his mind.

"Good, not in the mood for a fight tonight. Management frowns on the bouncers starting them."

Bull leaned in and kissed the corner of his mouth, the tickle of Bull's beard teased his skin. As quick as Bull kissed him the man was gone.

"Should I get you some ice water to pour over your head," Twitch's teasing words came from behind him.

Gregory turned the stool back around. "Whatever do you mean?"

"Don't give me that shit. You got that man wrapped around your pinkie finger."

"Doubt it, but it's nice—"

"To be able to flirt, to just be without worrying about every word or move you make."

"Yeah, that."

With his permission, Bull shared what happened so the others could be on the lookout for trouble. Gregory hated they had to do that for him, yet it was nice to feel protected and cared about.

"The Twirled and Brawler Crews, especially this one may have tempers that would scare a sociopath, but the ones they care about they'd go to battle in a heartbeat."

"I'm not used to that."

"I wasn't either. When I started working here, fuck, I was scared shitless. I'm not exactly a fighter."

"Heard you can swing a mean bat though."

Twitch rolled his pretty eyes. "That was one time, and someone was going to knife Crave in the back. Everyone else was occupied. I didn't have a choice."

"I'm sure, isn't that when you two hooked up?"

"It was the final straw. He's such a caveman sometimes."

"Did it for ya, huh?"

"Bull's right, you're becoming one of us quick."

"Is that a bad thing?" Gregory asked.

He was still nervous about getting comfortable too quick. One day he was going to have to move on and leave the farm behind. Although, Gregory hoped he was always welcome and remained friends, especially with Bull.

"Not bad at all, seems like life has been more than a bit of a bitch lately."

Arnold was still making a nuisance of himself. There were calls and texts, Arnold had even come to the office a few more times, but Landon sent the man away. He'd made Landon promise not to tell Bull. Gregory hid in his office for hours before he'd felt safe enough to make a run to Bull's truck and head home.

"You can say that again."

"Also…" Twitch leaned on the bar "You could do so much worse than that sexy Daddy."

"Don't call him that, he hates it."

"Maybe." Twitch winked.

Twitch skipped away before he had a chance to ask what he meant. Gregory turned to lean against the wall and immediately searched Bull out. Bull was positioned across the room beside the door. His thick, muscled arms crossed over his chest. He didn't know why he was so fascinated with the thick hair covering Bull's arms and chest. Gregory had even noticed a small patch at the indent of his lower spine.

Hairy men were never his type, older men certainly weren't, and he hoped it wasn't some Knight in Scarred Leather obsession. Bull didn't have to come to his rescue or offer him a place in Bull's home, but he had. He was grateful, yet he didn't feel that was all there was to it.

Sleeping in Bull's bed the night before, even for a few hours, was the best sleep he'd had in months, maybe years. He'd woken up with his face nuzzling Bull's chest and wrapped in Bull's arms. While Matty was asleep in the three-sided crib. Gregory hadn't felt safe in so long it overwhelmed him. He'd stayed as still as possible wanting just a minute to analyze it. He still didn't have an answer.

What the hell would he even do with a man like Bull? The question brought on ideas, but he could never go through with them. Seduction wasn't his strong suit. Arnold hadn't had sex with him in forever, not since Arnold started taking his ring off. Their sex life had always been a bit—mechanical. Scheduled, Arnold would finish, take a shower and when he go to bed, he'd turned his back to Gregory.

Arnold hadn't even liked to kiss him. He shook his head and turned his gaze back to Bull to find the man watching him. Bull raised a brow as if to ask was he alright. Gregory smiled in answer. He was fine, Gregory only hoped it stayed that way.

9 BULL WAS EVICTING THEM ALL

Bull just dropped off the custom order, and he tried to stretch out the twinge in his lower back as he pulled in next to his workshop. When he'd left the house, the only one up and gone was Twitch to do the weekly shopping for everyone. He swore they wouldn't know what to do without Twitch. The little man ran the house like a drill sergeant and made no apologies for it.

If everyone's list wasn't tacked on the board next to the grocery list, they were shit-outta-luck unless they shopped themselves. He had to admit they'd gotten a little lazy with Twitch taking over like he did. Bull got out and slammed the door behind him as he made his way across the yard.

He climbed the three steps to the back door and opened it, then stepped inside. Everyone was sitting around the kitchen table including Gregory. He was working from home more than going to the office. The guys were snickering, but Gregory's face was bright red as he looked everywhere but at Bull.

"What the fuck did y'all do," he growled.

Which only made the guys' chuckling turn to loud belly laughs until they had tears streaming down their faces.

Twitch was innocently unpacking groceries and placing their personal items in plastic baskets. A new box of condoms and a large bottle of lube set right on top of his. He closed his eyes as he dropped his head back and focused on not killing them.

"I'm going to kill you all."

"But, Bull, better safe than sorry and really, man, you can only—"

"You're all evicted, get out of my house," he yelled as he lowered his head and glared at all of them.

"Oh please, you'd never kick Twitch out," Crave piped up from his perch on the counter. "And we're a package deal."

Bull groaned, he'd never kick them out. They'd called his bluff countless times over the years.

"And those are too small," Bull pointed at the condoms.

"What the hell do you mean too small?"

Twitch picked up the box and Bull raised a brow.

"Those are more your boy's size."

"It can't be that—"

Bull raised his hands and started undoing his belt, popped the button on his jeans, and had his zipper halfway down.

"No, that be like seeing my dad's dick," Twitch screeched. "I can't believe you almost pulled it out in the kitchen, this my kitchen, Bull, mine."

"Like you and Crave ain't gone at it on my kitchen table more than once."

"That was one time, and everyone should have been asleep." Crave jumped down from the counter.

"I got some more your size, ya know, if the time comes," Psycho nodded toward Gregory.

The man still wasn't looking at any of them, and Gregory seemed to be mentally searching for a happy place. If Bull wasn't mistaken though, the man darted glances out of the corner of his eye at Bull's partially undone pants. Bull was seconds away from pulling a caveman and tossing Gregory over his shoulder.

He's wanted to get Gregory naked since the first night he'd met him at Brawlers. The need only grew more over the last month Gregory was under his roof.

"You're a real friend, Psycho. Who the fuck wants to go a few rounds?"

"I'm in." Psycho was out of his chair before he stopped talking.

Of course Psycho would be the first to take the challenge.

"You can't break my nose twice in a row."

Psycho was still holding a grudge about the last time they burned off their anger. He'd had the boxing ring put in not long after he started taking in the strays. Fighting amongst themselves outside the confines of the ring was against the rules. He had a three strikes you're out policy around there.

"Who the fuck says I can't," Bull asked.

"Me, because that was a cheap fucking shot. Now do up your jeans, I ain't kicking your ass with your dick hanging out. Besides you're embarrassing the newbie."

"Fine, get the right size next time, Twitch."

"Can we stop talking about your monster dick?" Twitch busied himself putting away the last of the groceries. "I'm traumatized already."

"Next time play your jokes on someone else." He did up his zipper and secured his belt.

"Sufficiently chastised."

"Cheering section?"

"We're in, Gregory hasn't experienced a Battle at Brawlers Farm yet."

Bull looked at Gregory and hated the way he wrung his hands. "Everyone out, we'll be in the barn in a few."

For once everyone listened, and he was left alone with Gregory. He approached and crouched down in front of him.

"Hey, what's this?" Bull took Gregory's hands in his to keep him from twisting his fingers too hard.

"You were getting ready to—"

He suppressed his smile as Gregory motioned toward his crouch. Bull didn't like Gregory's embarrassment. The man fitted in so well they didn't actually think about some of their shit making him uncomfortable. He brought Gregory's hands to his mouth and brushed his lips across his knuckles.

"No, I wasn't, Twitch would've fallen right out. If you don't want to watch the fight, you don't have to come out."

"Do y'all fight often?"

Maybe the threat of violence was bothering him more than the other thing now. "Too much testosterone living under the same roof sometimes things get out of hand. The rule is, no one can fight outside the ring."

"So, there's rules?"

"Not really, other than don't cause serious damage. Gloves, no bare-knuckle brawls. I'm getting way too old, and I don't heal as fast as I used to. Remember, grumpy old man?"

Thankfully Gregory's lips stretched into a small smile. "Will it bother you if I don't watch?"

"No, I'm sure you have some work to do or just take advantage of not having to share the remote."

"That would be great."

"Or you can come out and cheer this old man on, while everyone calls for Psycho to take me down."

"They'd do that?"

"Every damn time. No respect for their elders."

"You're not that old."

"Thanks."

Gregory jerked his hands from his and pushed Bull's chest. He didn't resist and fell onto his ass.

"You know what I meant."

Bull leaned back on his hands and looked up at Gregory. The man smiled, and his face wasn't flushed.

"Are those condoms really too small?"

"Yep," Bull answered with a grin.

His supposed endowment was a long-standing joke because of his nickname, but Gregory didn't know that, and it was too fun to tease the other man.

"You're such an asshole."

"And you're just now realizing that means I must be losing my edge."

"Since I'm living here now, I should, you know, take part in Brawler customs, right?"

"No inside the ring for you." Bull didn't care if the man got insulted by his order, but there wasn't a chance he'd let Gregory get hurt.

"Would you teach me though?"

Gregory wasn't violent by any stretch of the imagination, but from the expression on the man's beautiful face, he knew Gregory needed to know how. No matter what he hoped, someone wouldn't always be around to protect Gregory. His resources only stretched so far.

"I can do that. Come on and watch the fight, then afterward I'll show you a few things."

He got to his feet and held his hand out to Gregory. Bull led Gregory from the house and toward the barn. "Warning, it's gonna be brutal, but remember we're all friends and family here. Just a release of tension…sometimes anger."

"Are you going to get your ass kicked?"

"Hey, have a little fucking faith in me. I may be older, but dammit, I'm wiser and have more experience. Experience has its perks."

"I'm sure it does."

Bull didn't know if he was talking about Bull's fighting or bedroom technique. He wasn't going to let his brain go there. He released Gregory's hand and stripped off his t-shirt. He held out his hands as Crave started taping them and Twitch stood nearby with gloves.

"I'll take care of him while you're getting your ass kicked," Twitch said with an evil glint in his eye.

For somewhat of a pacifist, Twitch was a vicious little shit.

"Don't take care of him too much, that's my job."

"Why you think I got you the supplies," Twitch winked. "Kisses for luck, come here you, crazy asshole."

Bull laughed as Twitch reached up and grabbed Psycho's face, then dragged the man down to brush a kiss across his cheek.

"Where's mine," Bull asked.

"Uh huh, my money's on Psycho."

"Ouch…" Bull grabbed his chest and staggered backward. "I'm wounded."

Twitch rolled his eyes. "Doubt it."

"Do you see how they treat me?" Bull asked Gregory.

"It's a crime."

"You youngsters have no respect. We doing this or not?" Bull stepped toward the ring but stopped when Gregory grabbed his wrist. He turned to see if he needed to ease Gregory's fears. Soft lips pressed to his and hands settled at his waist, then Gregory pulled back.

"For luck," Gregory whispered as he stepped away.

He instantly wanted Gregory back and turn the innocent kiss into something more. Audience be damned, but he made his decision with his head, not his heart or dick. "Thanks."

"You're welcome."

A huge hand slapped his back, and he glanced over his shoulder. He suddenly didn't want to work off months' worth of frustration by fighting, but in his bed with Gregory's lean body beneath him. Bull needed Gregory to beg for his cock.

"Head in the game, old man, and not on your man's ass," Psycho whispered.

"Easy for you to say."

All talking ceased as Psycho and he circled each other. Cheers filled the space between fists connecting with flesh, heavy breathing, and grunts. The brutality of battle he understood, and he lost himself in it. An exchanging of punches and kicks, the pain, and adrenaline. If he couldn't have what and who he wanted, he could work for a chance of victory.

10 GREGORY CAN HIDE ONLY SO LONG

Gregory turned up the music on his laptop as he got up and poured another cup of coffee. He didn't realize how much work he could get done at home. Three projects finished ahead of schedule, and the courier already picked up the packages. He lifted onto his toes and leaned forward to peek out the window.

Bull's truck that Gregory used was parked in its usual spot, and Bull's motorcycle was still there. He checked the time and figured Bull would be up by then. With all the guys working that night he'd made sure he was quiet since he had to get up early to work.

One of his favorite songs came on, slow and bluesy. He closed his eyes and lower his chin to his chest. As much as he loved it there, it was getting harder to live under Bull's roof. It was like constant temptation. Twitch screwed with his head with the condoms and lube prank. Since then, all he could think about was finding out what Bull almost exposed the other day. The thick nest of curls and just the hint of the thick base.

Gregory groaned. He was sure Bull only saw him as a friend. They flirted and sometimes he swore he caught Bull watching him. He jerked his head up and spun as he heard the song restart. Bull stood beside the kitchen table. He was dressed for work in jeans, boots and a Brawlers Security t-shirt. His hair damp.

Bull held out his hand and raised a brow in silent question.

Gregory smiled and reached out, he was spun deftly into Bull's arms.

"Now, where did you learn that," Gregory asked as he loosely looped his arms around Bull's neck.

"Polly loved to dance."

The mention of Bull's ex-wife didn't bother him. He knew the man loved Polly as a friend, maybe his best one. Gregory knew it would never happen, but he wished he'd meet the woman one day.

He followed Bull's lead as the big man moved him gracefully around the floor. That's when he became aware of things he shouldn't—like the hard muscles of Bull's chest. The firm muscled curve of Bull's stomach conformed to his softer stomach. He absently caressed the roughness of the buzzed hair at the back of Bull's head.

Gregory closed his eyes and pressed his face into the curve of Bull's neck, he inhaled Bull's scent. Took the comforting mix of soap and man into his lungs. Bull's strong fingers kneaded the small of his back and seemed to tug him closer. The roughness of Bull's beard stroked along his cheek, and Gregory lifted his head. He held his breath as Bull's teased his lips.

All he had to do was tilt his chin and Bull's mouth would be on his. Bull's hands tightened on his waist. He opened his eyes to find Bull watching him. The tension built and his heartbeat kicked up to the point he heard the blood rushing in his ears. He sighed, and Bull started to close the few inches of space between them.

"This is where the hell you're—oh, shit."

Landon's voice had them jumping apart.

"Didn't mean to interrupt, I can come back—"

Landon had a wicked grin on his face, and he knew he was on for it when they were alone.

"No, I'll let you two work, I gotta get going. The rest of the crew are getting their shit together."

Gregory noticed Bull was looking everywhere but at him. He forced a smile as he caught Landon studying him. Bull appeared not to be able to get away fast enough, but he paused long enough to kiss Landon's cheek before he headed for the back door.

The screen door slammed, and Gregory fell into the nearest chair.

"I'm sorry, if I'd noticed I would've left."

"Nothing was going on. It was just a dance, no big deal."

"Oh, that was a big damn deal," Landon said and took the seat nearest him.

"No—"

"If I'm not mistaken, and I know I'm not, you and Bull were about to kiss. When did this happen? I mean the crews been talking about you two, but I just thought they were talking shit. Bull's not exactly your type."

"What's that mean?"

"Well, blue collar, bad boy, and a helluva lot older."

He was getting tired of the older thing. So what if Bull was twenty years his senior, but the man was sexy as hell. Fuck, he could still feel the impression of Bull's big body against his, and he'd wanted more, still did. "He's not that old."

"Um, Gregory, can I ask you something?"

"What?"

"Do you have a thing about Daddies?"

Gregory rolled his eyes. "Why is everyone asking me that?"

"Kinky."

"Shut up."

He wasn't kinky. He was vanilla as it got. Before Arnold and he stopped having sex, it was maybe once every two weeks or month. He didn't even enjoy it.

Landon laughed and leaned back in the chair.

"So, want to talk about it?"

He shouldn't, but other than the Brawlers Crew, Landon was really his only friend. Gregory was friendly with the Twirled guys as well. He needed to talk it out because, to be honest, he was completely losing it.

"I'm in over my head here."

"How so?"

"He's gorgeous."

"He doesn't think so, I've heard he said he's a bit homely."

"He's insane. He's gorgeous. Caring."

"Possessive. Packing several inches of thick prime—"

Gregory glared and felt his hands clench into fists.

"Oh, jealous."

"I'd prefer if you didn't talk about—"

"His dick."

He didn't appreciate Landon's laughter. Gregory was never a jealous man, but the thought of someone else seeing—it wasn't his business.

"What you gonna do about you lusting after our resident Daddy?"

"Nothing. I'm still married, remember?"

"You're separated, people that are separated date all the time."

"If Arnold ever—"

"I think the moment Bull told Arnold you were his and don't fuck with what's his, you worrying about Arnold finding out is a lost fucking cause. I heard about what happened at Twirled. Bull said you belonged in his bed."

"I can't believe he did that." Gregory buried his face in his hands.

"A bit of advice, I've known Bull for years and the rest of the crew, their possessive as hell. They stake their ownership loud and proud."

Gregory lifted his head. "Bull doesn't own me." That shouldn't make him depressed. What was wrong with him?

"Not yet, but once he gets you in bed, you're not getting away."

"See, that's the thing, I should be running. Arnold–"

"Arnold is an abusive asshole. Bull is nothing of the sort. Yeah, he's got a temper, but no way would he ever do to you or anyone what that bastard did. He even came to your rescue, maybe it's just—"

"It's not gratitude. Yeah, I appreciate what he's done. Offering me a home here. I love it here."

"Then why fight it so hard. Just see what happens."

"What if I'm seeing things."

"You're definitely not seeing things. Like I said, I've known Bull for ten years, and in all that time, I've never seen him like he is since you moved in. You're good for the cranky bastard, as a friend or a lover."

"I'm just terrified. Arnold keeps trying to see me. He's calling and sending texts. I've blocked his numbers, and it doesn't work."

"Have you told Bull?"

"No."

"You should. Him and the guys should be aware if trouble's coming."

"Okay, I'll talk to him when he gets home."

"You're up when he gets home?" Landon's brow rose.

"Yeah, most days I get up about one like everyone else."

"Wow, you're becoming a Brawler. Is that why you've been working from home?"

"Not really. I get so much more done here than at the office."

"Speaking of the office, you got a few minutes to talk about a couple of clients that called?"

"Yeah, want some coffee?"

"Sure."

"Shit, Bull didn't get his coffee before he left. Twitch," Gregory yelled as he poured Landon a mug, then carried it to the table.

"You bellowed?" Twitch skipped into the room already dressed. "Hey, Landon."

"Twitch."

"Bull left, and he didn't get his coffee."

"Thanks for the heads up. Making him a thermos? He likes your coffee better than mine."

"Yeah, I'll be ready by the time y'all leave."

"Staying for breakfast, Landon?"

"Twitch, normal people have lunch or early dinner about this time."

"This ain't a normal family."

Gregory only half listened to the conversation as the rest of the Brawler Crew joined them. He brewed a fresh pot of coffee to fill a thermos. Bull liked his coffee strong enough to strip paint.

His mind went back to the almost kiss. Was it real or was he just imagining what he wanted to see? Gregory was quickly coming to the point he didn't know if he could resist doing something stupid. If he embarrassed himself in front of Bull, he'd lose him and the place he was quickly calling home. These people were weird, but they were his family, and he loved every crazy one of them, but what he felt for Bull was different. He didn't want to name it or even think about it. He was already too far gone to stop it. Resisting was his only option, and the very thought of not having Bull already killed him. What would happen if he let things get out of hand? Would he even survive it?

11 AN EMPTY HOUSE WAS A
DANGEROUS THING

Brawlers was closed on Sundays, so that meant everyone would be hanging around the house. Bull walked out of his bedroom roughly pushing his fingers through his hair. He needed coffee. He'd spent most of the fucking night thinking about the almost kiss. So close, barely a breath separated their mouths, and he could've tasted Gregory for real. Nowhere near the innocent corner of the mouth kiss at the bar or the good luck one from the fight the other night.

He just didn't know if he saw shit or if the man actually wanted him. There was also the fucked-up situation of Gregory's ex. It was already three in the afternoon. He hadn't crashed until well after sunrise but resisted sitting on the front porch. It was a chicken shit move to avoid Gregory. The man sensed when he was outside and always came to join him.

He jogged down the steps and toward the kitchen, then he realized the house was too quiet. No fighting. No threats of bloodshed. No loud sex. The coffee pot was full, and his mug was sitting in front of it.

It was fucking weird. He poured himself some coffee, then headed for the living room. He stopped in the doorway at the sight of Gregory on the couch. The man's laptop balanced on his crossed legs. Gregory had black framed reading glasses perched on the end of his nose. Fuck, that was sexy, no, not sexy. *Shit.*

"Where are heathens?" he asked as he strode toward the couch.

"Well, Twitch and Crave left not long after they came home to head to Tank's cabin for a night alone. They said they'd be back tomorrow." Gregory closed his laptop and leaned forward to place it on the coffee table. "Hunter got permission from his probation officer to go visit his parents, so he'll be back tomorrow sometime before work. When I was outside earlier, I saw the faint outline of Ben being mauled while bent over Psycho's bike. I could've done without that one. Voices carry way too much, or his screams were just that loud."

"Nice morning."

Bull snorted at the unimpressed look Gregory was giving him while glaring at him over his glasses.

"I can deal with sex here, I can put my earbuds in and drown it out, but it's another to hear what Psycho was saying. Porn would be considered PG compared to...I almost started drinking."

Bull laughed and fell back on the couch, he turned his head to look at Gregory. "Imagine them just across the yard."

"I'm horrified to even imagine. That man is nasty, and I'll never be able to look at him again."

He had to admit Psycho probably had dirty talk down to an art form. If by the whimpers, screams, and begging that went on in the trailer Ben hadn't minded at all.

"If this is your first time walking in or seeing the married ones going at it, you're lucky. I nearly laid Crave out when I caught him and Twitch, I thought he was hurting the kid."

"That's bad. Don't call Twitch a kid, he doesn't like it," Gregory admonished as he turned to tuck his legs under him and lay his arm on the back of the couch.

Bull shrugged. "It's why I do it."

"Y'all live to give each other shit."

"Yes, we do. Makes life more interesting. Speaking of interesting, you're working on a Sunday, normally this is your reading your trashy romance on your e-reader days." He pointed to the offending device in question.

"It's not trashy, it's very well written."

"Whatever you say."

"Don't even start. I hadn't been able to do a lot of reading until I moved here. And the last thing I saw you read was the newspaper."

"Yeah, I'm old, I read the newspaper and drink my coffee, speaking of which where is it?"

"Twitch wasn't here to get you one."

"How the hell am I supposed to relax?"

"Um, borrow my e-reader?"

"No, that's okay. Not really the romance type."

"Why don't you take yours out of the box and just download your paper? Twitch bitches he got it for you, and you don't even use it."

"It's not the same. You don't get the smell of ink or black on your fingertips, and your little device doesn't have the satisfying snap of the paper when you're warning the heathens to shut the fuck up."

"You're so old."

Gregory laid his head on his arm and rolled his eyes. A smile teased the corners of Gregory's mouth, and that wasn't something he should focus on. Gregory's mouth was off-limits, everything about Gregory was not for him.

"Thanks for pointing out the obvious."

"Quit being an ass because you don't have your paper. What are your plans for the day?"

"Since I don't have my paper, I'm pretty much out of options."

"You going to complain about that the rest of the evening," Gregory asked.

"Probably." Then a thought struck him. "You want to go for a ride?"

"Really?"

"Yeah, maybe grab some dinner."

"I'm pretty much done with work. Where would we go?"

"Nowhere in particular, but there's this great steakhouse. It's a few hours ride away, but it's a great trip. We can get ready and head out, can be there for dinner."

"You don't mind, I know you like to relax—"

"Wouldn't have asked if it wasn't and you seemed to like the last time I took you out."

"It's amazing. I loved it."

"Okay, get your ass up and ready. I'll jump in the shower and be ready in about thirty."

"Okay." Gregory jumped up and headed for the steps.

Bull took a few more swallows of his coffee and curled up to get to his feet. He heard Gregory's door close as he ascended the steps. A ride sounded like a good idea, and it got them out of the house. Unless it was work or Brawlers, Gregory didn't leave the house, he'd even started working from home and only going in for meetings. He had a feeling it had more to do with Arnold than liking being at home.

He walked into his room and closed the door behind him. Bull could only do so much to help if Gregory didn't tell him what was going on. Arnold seemed like the type to do whatever he could to hurt Gregory. It was also a selfish way for Bull to get more time with the man. They'd spent a lot of time together in the weeks Gregory lived there and talked. He relished his friendship with Gregory, and as much as he didn't want to fuck it up, he didn't know how much longer he could resist making the man his.

He grabbed clothes and headed for the shower. He had twenty minutes to meet Gregory downstairs.

■■■■

They'd had dinner and just started on dessert. Gregory's smile was bright, a bit from laughter and some from the wine Gregory had. He had to talk Gregory into having wine with his dinner. Luckily, it hadn't turned into a battle. He didn't pretend he wasn't a former drunk and it didn't bother him when people drank around him. If it did, he wouldn't work at Brawlers.

"Crave didn't?" Gregory laughed as he picked at his cheesecake.

"I swear that boy's brains are in his dick. He threatened any man who even looked at Twitch."

"But taunting them until they swung first just so he could—"

"Kick their asses without getting in trouble, yeah he did. I'd known about it awhile, but he generally went after guys that were assholes."

"But how did Psycho and Ben get together, that's a weird combo."

"Elijah and Landon swore they were going to do a Brawlers Dating 101 class. Psycho hasn't changed much over the months since him and Ben had gotten together. The story is…" Bull took a sip of his water, "Elijah told Psycho he needed to get out more. So he went to the new bakery in town. The girl that worked for Ben pushed open the door while he was spying on Psycho. She bloodied his nose."

"Really?"

"Yeah, so while Ben is sitting there with a tampon up his nose, Psycho basically asked the man home to fuck."

"And why doesn't that surprise me," Gregory asked and took a bite of cheesecake.

Bull nearly groaned as Gregory slowly slid the fork from between his lips then ran his tongue along his upper one. Shit, the man was going give him a hard-on in the middle of the fucking restaurant.

"Yeah, Psycho isn't the smoothest man around, but him and Ben just fit."

"What about you, no dating?"

"Not much. Don't really want to get involved with customers. Shit goes south, and it brings drama. What about you?"

Gregory sighed and laid his fork on his plate. "My dating history is abysmal."

"Why, you're gorgeous, fun, great sense of humor if at sometimes twisted, but I think that's from being around us too much."

"Probably true, but, I don't know, I put so much time into school and then getting my business going. Dating took a backseat. The ones I did date grew bored and decided to find someone more exciting even before they broke up with me. I was never the bars or clubs type. My parents were pretty strict growing up."

"Strict?"

"Not mean or anything like that, but education was important, and they didn't want anything getting in the way." Gregory rested his elbows on the table and rested his clasped hands under his chin. "They both couldn't afford college and worked shitty jobs just to pay the bills. They put away every dime they could for my schooling, but me going to college depended on scholarships. That wasn't going to happen if I slacked and they wanted better for me."

"I get that."

"What about Hank?"

"He followed in my footsteps, joined the Marines, and they paid for his school. He wasn't the best student. Smart as fuck, just easily bored. He turned the military into his career."

"Just like you?"

"I put in twenty years. Polly wasn't happy when he said he joined. That was a fight. The three of us spent hours going around, but he was eighteen and an adult."

"How did he feel when you came out?"

"The hard questions." Bull laughed. "He didn't get how I could stay married to his mom for twenty-five years and pretend to be someone I wasn't."

"But you loved her."

"Yeah, I still do. When you're with someone for almost thirty years, you can't just turn it off. Even if there were more bad times than good, we always remained friends even if our farce of a romantic relationship was shit."

"Do you see them a lot?"

"Not much, mostly emails, phone calls on holidays, but when Hank's home on leave we always get together for dinner. Which he'll be home in a few weeks, I'll be going to Tampa for a week."

"A week?"

"Yeah, you heathens will be without supervision, just don't destroy my house while I'm gone."

"It won't be the same."

"We do need to talk about something though." Bull leaned his forearms on the table.

"Don't ruin the night, Bull."

"I won't be there, so I have to—"

"He's still calling, texting, even came to the office a few times."

"Why the fuck didn't you tell me?" His voice rose, and then he looked around to make sure no one was watching. Maybe a public restaurant wasn't the place to have this conversation.

"I thought he'd grow bored by now."

"Apparently, that's not what's happening, you're coming with me."

"What, coming where?"

"To see Polly and Hank, you can hang on the beach and have a vacation."

"I can't intrude on your trip."

"I know you want to meet Polly. You're curious, and she has a ton of embarrassing stories I'm sure she'd love to share."

"That's a bit of incentive. I haven't been to the beach in forever. Arnold always wanted Paris, Rome and all those types of places."

"Then it's settled, I'll buy you a ticket when I get mine this week."

"I'll pay."

"No, I got it, no arguments."

He knew arguments were coming. The man agreed way too quick to coming with him, yet he knew it would do Gregory good to get out of Powers for a bit. To not have to worry about looking over his shoulder while going to work or the store. He also wanted Polly and Gregory to meet. Bull had a strong feeling they'd like each other.

"Fine, but there's something I wanted to ask you, but never knew how."

"Ask anything."

"What's your real name?"

"That's all you want to know, my name."

"Yeah, you've never told me, and everyone just calls you Bull."

"Archer."

"Archer," Gregory repeated, "I like it."

He liked the way his name sounded on Gregory's lips. He wanted to hear it again, but he already got enough shit for his undeniable attraction to Gregory. No one was oblivious except Gregory.

"Thanks. I think Polly's the only one who still calls me it. She's even started calling me Bull."

"Why Bull?"

This wasn't going to be a pretty story, but he did say Gregory could ask anything.

"Short for Bulletproof. Not long after I got the job at Brawlers. Some guy who didn't like the gays in his town came in wielding a 12-gauge. Let's just say Bulletproof was a misnomer."

"He shot you?"

"Twice, punctured a lung and nicked my liver."

"I didn't see any scars."

"Did you see the amount of hair? They're hidden in the overgrowth."

"I don't think you should joke about some bastard trying to kill you."

Gregory sounded cute when he was all offended on his behalf.

"Yeah, but I survived, and it wasn't the first time someone tried to kill me. I'm a bit of an asshole."

"I don't think you are. You're a bit gruff but exceptionally charming."

"Charming, that's a new one."

"Probably, but your prickly nature disguises it."

"A compliment followed by an insult to my personality. You're so sweet."

"I try."

"You ready to head out and get home?"

"Yeah, I was up early and getting a little tired. The cool night air will help wake me up some."

Bull raised his hand to call the server over. The woman approached with a warm smile, he reached back to pull out his wallet and slipped his card into the padded binder with the check. He ignored Gregory's protests that he wanted to pay half. He winked at the server, and she giggled as she rushed off pretending to not hear Gregory trying to call her back.

"I want to know how much so I can pay."

"No, my idea, my treat, get the fuck over it."

"I take back the charming compliment," Gregory huffed.

"Pout all you want, I ain't telling you how much dinner was."

"Fine, but next time is on me."

"Deal," Bull lied.

Gregory narrowed his eyes but didn't say anything. The man could glare all he wanted, Bull got his way, and that's all he cared about. The server returned, he signed the slip, gave her a generous tip.

"Your boyfriend's really cute," she whispered.

"Yeah, he is," he said as he handed her the folder back.

"Have a good night."

Bull stood then walked around to pull Gregory's chair out. He didn't give a fuck who was watching, he kept his hand on Gregory's lower back as he led him toward the exit, then outside.

"Thanks for dinner."

"You're welcome. It's been awhile. It was nice to get out of town for a bit. Thanks for coming with me."

He mounted his bike and waited while Gregory got on. The man rested his feet on the pegs and scooted close, wrapping his body around Bull's. He could too easily get used to that and not just Gregory riding with him. It hadn't been two months yet and the part of his brain he tried to ignore formulated a life with Gregory. Too old or not, he knew he couldn't just put Gregory in the friend category. He wanted more, but he had to make sure Gregory was ready, and Arnold was out of the way.

Bull wasn't a man that lived a half-life. When he got Gregory, and it was when and not if, he just hoped he didn't fuck up Gregory's life as much as he had Polly's for so many years. He started the bike, listening to the soothing rumble, and Gregory pushed even closer until Bull was cradled fully between the man's lean, muscled legs. He took off toward home with his man cuddled to his back and plans formed in his head.

12 WHY WAS GREGORY SO NERVOUS TO MEET HER?

Two weeks flew by, and Gregory was about to get off a plane and meet Bull's ex-wife. He'd tried to get out of it, made every excuse he could, and none of them worked. Bull wasn't taking no for an answer. Gregory had to admit he needed a vacation, a week without work and maybe some time to lay on the beach.

"You're about to have a fucking panic attack, relax," Bull whispered in his ear.

He closed his eyes as the man's beard brushed his throat. *Don't lean in, don't lean*—he ruined it as he turned his head and Bull's mouth brushed against his cheek. He was definitely becoming obsessed with hairy men, well, only one. Bull bumped his jaw with his nose, Gregory tilted his head, so his temple rested to Bull's forehead.

It was getting harder not to finish what he thought they'd started in the kitchen. Even before that, he loved flirting with the older man.

"I'm trying, but it's her, and I'm nervous."

"Don't be, Polly's the most down to earth person I know. Remember this is supposed to be a vacation."

"I know."

"Come on, if we take too long she'll run passed security to hunt us down."

Gregory rolled his eyes as Bull stood and held out his hand. He didn't hesitate to take it. The rough callouses were almost as sexy as the beard and hair covered chest. He loathed when Bull wore a shirt. He hadn't even seen the man fully naked yet, but he knew it was a crime to cover all that sexiness up.

He could see it now if Landon was there, he'd be giving Gregory hell. Bull tugged, and Gregory stood, the bigger man didn't release his hand as he pulled down their backpacks from the overhead. He took his bag, then Bull slung his own over his broad shoulder. There was something about the man not caring who saw him holding Gregory's hand.

They disembarked and walked through the tunnel. He noticed a few people passing them and giving them looks, but he couldn't make himself give a shit. For a little while, he wanted to pretend the man was his.

The tunnel opened up into the terminal. People loitered on the other side of the ropes. He scanned the crowd and didn't have to search too long for Polly. A beautiful woman with dark blonde hair and a gently rounded face smiled as she waved her arms over her head. A tall, distinguished man was grinning at her with eyes that showed the love he had for her.

"Archer," Polly screamed as she pushed sideways through the crowd.

He released Bull's hand as the man took three long strides and swept her up in his arms. Gregory laughed at the loud sound of a kiss on her neck and then her boisterous laughter.

"Archer, dammit, I'm a married woman."

"A sexy, beautiful married woman."

He snorted as Bull growled and proceeded to tickle her neck with his beard. That was definitely new. He stood back and let them have their moment.

"Hal, how ya doing, man," Bull asked as he moved Polly to his side to shake the man's hand.

"Doing good, Archer, glad you could make it."

"Now, who's this?"

He was suddenly the center of attention as gorgeous blue eyes locked onto him. Gregory instantly liked her just from the happiness in her eyes. The lines beside them spoke of years of smiles.

"Polly, this is Gregory, Gregory, this is Polly." Bull leaned down. "He was terrified to meet you."

"Bull, don't be an asshole."

"I like him already, hello, Gregory, if he doesn't treat you right I'll kick his ass."

"That I'd love to see. He hasn't lost a fight since I moved in."

"Moved in?" She turned to level a curious stare at Bull. "And why didn't this come up in any of our texts?"

"It's ain't like that, darling, he has his own room."

"Losing your touch, something that sexy living in my house I would've jumped him already."

Gregory couldn't help it he lost it and loudly laughed.

"Yeah, yeah, leave it alone."

"Archer, that glare stopped working on me about a year after we started dating."

Bull heavily sighed, "Yeah, I know. When's Hank getting in?"

"Delayed flight, he'll be arriving on a red eye."

"Shit, well, at least that'll give Gregory time to get used to you first before the other insane one arrives."

"I'll make sure to tell Hank that."

"Snitch. Come on, baby, let's get our bags."

Polly did a perfect twirl on her toes to face Gregory again and mouthed baby with a perfectly arched brow. He was saved from questions as Hal stepped up.

"Since the rude ones aren't going to introduce us, I'm Hal."

"Nice to meet you, I've heard a lot about both of you, and Hank."

"We can't say the same, shall we?" Hal held out his elbow.

He slipped his arm through Hal's and swore he heard a growl behind him as Hal tugged him along to baggage claim.

"Polly and Archer act like old friends when they get together. Takes them about an hour to acknowledge anyone else."

"Does that bother you? Shit, I shouldn't have asked."

"No big deal, I learned pretty quick Polly was a package deal, that included Hank and Archer. He's had a hard time of it as I'm sure you're probably aware. Took a bit longer to warm up to Archer."

"He has his moments that's for sure."

"Nice way of putting it. Been dating long?"

The depth of the need to say they were dating shocked him for a moment. He wanted more, and sometimes he thought Bull did as well, but nothing went passed their friendly relationship. He'd lost count of how many times he'd set on a Brawlers barstool and watched Bull work all night, then he'd savor his ride home on the back of Bull's bike.

"No, just friends, I'm recently separated."

"Sorry to hear that."

"Don't be, was definitely for the best. Landon—"

"How is Landon?"

"He's great, he's running the office for me while I'm out of town. I see you know him and Bull are friends. Bull offered me a place to stay while I get the divorce taken care of."

"It's good to have friends, and last time we visited Powers, the farm was definitely the place to be."

"Free ringside seats most weekends." He laughed with Hal. "I'm getting pretty good at skin glue, still won't do the stitches though."

"No need to be, Twitch is a pro."

He felt Bull brush against him and step forward to grab Gregory's suitcase and his duffel. Gregory pulled away from Hal to step forward to take his bag from Bull.

"I got it," Bull said and leaned forward to brush a kiss to the corner of Gregory's mouth.

Man, Bull needed to stop doing that. It kept fucking with his head.

"You sure, I mean you're not as young as you used to be."

"Oh, now you got jokes about the old man. I see your devotion was short lived."

"Shut up, big man, prove your manliness and carry the damn bags."

"I will."

He snorted as Bull walked off carrying everything. Gregory just stood watching him leave. His gaze dropped to Bull's firm ass perfectly showed off in jeans. It was getting imposable not to think about cupping it as Bull pounded—he shook his head and followed Bull.

"He's very stubborn," Polly's voice came from his right.

He turned to look at her. "You're not telling me anything new. I learned that pretty quick."

"He's looking good. The last time he was here he was all scowls for a few days. It sounds like you've been good for him."

The message in Polly's voice was evident, but he didn't want her to get the wrong idea. "He's become a friend over the last few months."

"Now, I'm an old, wise woman and I know there isn't all friends-only playing in that gorgeous head of yours."

"That's all there is."

He hoped that would be the end of it.

"Let's get home and get y'all settled. My stepdaughters are away at college, so it'll be fun to have a full house again."

He was thankful for the reprieve. In his gut, he knew that wasn't the end of it, but he'd deal with that as it came. Quickly they were in the car and headed toward Hal and Polly's house.

■■■■

An hour later, Gregory was settled into a room that overlooked the beach and stood at the window. Bull and he had their first fight since landing when Gregory tried to take the pull-out couch in the den, so Bull could have the bedroom. He'd prefer if Bull shared. The man put out some heat and Gregory was always cold at night.

Bull sharing the bed with him would be too much temptation. He was already quickly losing his resolve. Bull was perfect, caring, protective, handsome beyond belief, Gregory even liked his surliness and his penchant for fighting. The good and bad just made up a package Gregory really wanted.

"I was wondering where you were," Bull asked.

The man's big body pressed up against his. There wasn't much difference in their height and Bull's chin easily rested on his shoulder.

"This view is incredible."

"Want to take a walk later on the beach when all the day people are sleeping?"

"Yes, but wouldn't it be rude for us to keep to our regular schedule?"

"Polly doesn't stand on ceremony around here. Besides, I may get up early, but you can sleep as late as you want. Vacation remember?"

"Yeah, but—"

"No buts, and if I see you check your email even once and I'll redden your ass."

The thought of Bull spanking him did unexpected things to his stomach and definitely lower. He'd been spanked once back in college, and it had been an awkward experience, not sexy in the least. He had a feeling that wouldn't be the case with Bull doing it.

"Threats are beneath you, Mr. Woods."

"Ew, Mr. Woods, low blow. Don't make an old man feel older."

"You're not old."

"Yes, I am, twenty years older than you. I was married with a kid before you were even born."

"And," Gregory asked.

Was that why Bull wouldn't give him a chance because Bull thought he was too young? At first, he'd worried about his attraction to the much older man, but no more. He thought the silver-haired bear was perfect.

"That means I'm old enough to be—"

"Shut up, Archer."

A silver streaked brow rose, and Gregory couldn't help snorting.

"Told you I liked your name."

"Yeah, but it sounds weird coming from you."

"Then maybe I'll use it just to give you a hard time."

"Not like you don't already. Polly threw together something for dinner and when I say threw the woman's been cooking for days. Hungry?"

"Starving, I've been spoiled by Twitch's cooking. Speaking of Twitch, did you call or text to let him know we got here?" Gregory asked as he stepped away from Bull and headed for the door.

"Yes, dear."

"Don't use that tone with me, Mr. Woods."

"You're fucking asking for it."

"Whatever do you mean," Gregory asked as he walked through the doorway listening to Bull mumbling behind him.

Apparently, Gregory Charles was learning to like living dangerously. He was going to make Archer "Bull" Woods his, and that's just what was going to happen. Gregory didn't care about Arnold. Didn't give a shit about the age difference. Safe, he was tired of being safe, what he wanted was the man coming up behind him. All he had to do was figure out how the hell to do it? He'd never claimed someone before, but he was sure going to give it a try.

13 THIS WASN'T GOING LIKE BULL PLANNED

Bull set on a beach chair as he watched the moon shimmer over the gentle waves. Too many years of working at the bar ruined his ability to sleep at night. Part of him hoped Gregory would join him, but a sleepless night and the flight had Gregory going to bed early.

"Still not sleeping at night, old man? Aren't you little old for the party all night shit?"

He surged to his feet and wrapped Hank in his arms. Hank was an exact younger version of him, except Hank's eyes were all Polly. He pushed Hank gently back to look at him. The lines beside Hank's eyes and mouth were deeper than the last time he'd seen his son. He definitely looked tired.

"Don't even say hello and already giving me shit."

"Did you expect anything else?"

"Not a damn chance, how was your trip?"

Hank stepped away and took the chair beside his, then let out a long weary sigh. Bull retook his seat as well.

"Long and one screw up after another. I never thought I'd get here."

"But you finally did make it."

The silence drew out between them as they stared off into the moonlit night.

Bull knew they'd avoid discussion of what happened while he was in country. None of them would push. He hadn't wanted the military life for Hank, but that had been his son's choice, and he wouldn't question it. Bull could only wish that if things went well with the woman his son was seeing, he'd take another course with his life.

"And do you know what I find out when I go to the guest room to jump on the bed like I used to when I was a kid."

"Oh, shit, did you wake Gregory?"

"If my reflexes weren't honed to perfection he would've stripped me of my manhood. For a pretty one, he's got a helluva kick."

"I should—"

"He said and I quote, tell the stubborn man not to check on me and spend time with you."

"Sounds like him. He was terrified to meet Polly."

"This is the first time we're meeting a boyfriend."

"Not a boyfriend, he's a friend. He's only been separated a few months. His husband was an asshole, and I told Gregory he was coming to live with me. I also said he needed a vacation and he was coming with me."

"You tell him what to do a lot, why does he put up with you?"

"I don't have much choice." Gregory leaned over the back of the chair.

He wondered how much of the conversation Gregory heard. He hadn't said anything that would hurt the man, so he didn't understand why he was worried.

"Damn right, what are you doing?"

"I figured you'd two wanted to catch up some, I brought coffee."

"Who drinks coffee in the middle of the night," Hank asked.

"It's only four a.m., and normally this is the time we're just relaxing for the evening. Here." Gregory moved between the chairs and extended the mugs.

He and Hank took them and thanked Gregory.

"You work with Dad?"

"Oh no, I'm a legal researcher. I've just gotten used to the hours, but I'm going to leave you two alone. Don't fall asleep out here, Bull, you'll be all cranky and stiff. Your poor old body and all."

Bull struck when Gregory turned to walk away and smacked Gregory's ass. "Don't be an asshole."

"I learned from the best," Gregory said and disappeared back toward the house.

"Spankings, and he's not your boyfriend?"

The amusement was thick in Hank's voice. He was thankful his son got Polly's personality because, to be honest, Bull didn't want Hank to turn out like him.

"The shit was asking for it."

"Uh-huh, whatever you say. You just wanted your hand on his ass."

"Shit," Bull groaned and tipped his head back.

"Does he know," Hank asked.

Bull didn't need to ask what Hank was talking about. He wouldn't even pretend he didn't know. The only answer he could give Hank was the truth.

"Way too young for me."

"How much younger?"

"You're older."

Hank let out a loud laugh. "Damn, robbing the cradle with that one."

"Thanks, and he accused me of being an asshole."

"What the hell is the problem?"

"His ex was abusive."

Bull didn't know if he could get passed that. He'd tried his best to keep his dominant personality under control. Yes, he was stubborn and bossy, he couldn't pretend he wasn't, but the things he wanted to do to Gregory couldn't occur.

"Did you take him out?"

"No, but I was damn tempted. Instead, I told him Gregory was mine and don't mess with him."

"Staking a claim, nice."

"I brought him here for a vacation so don't start interrogating him."

"Would I do that," Hank asked innocently.

"Yes, you would, both you and Polly are relentless."

"We just want you happy, it's been a long time since you could say that. And if we're honest with each other, have you ever been happy?"

"I was happy with you and Polly, just not in the way I could've been."

"Dad, you're gay, you love men, pretending to be some fucked up expectation of you ended up with you drinking away decades of your life. Mom's happy with Hal. It's about damn time you found someone of your own."

"I know, but his ex is an abusive fucker with a temper and addictions, not exactly sure if I'm a safe bet in the partner area."

106

"Safe is boring. Why don't you try this, ask him what he wants and quit assuming," Hank said.

"When the hell did you grow up?"

He loved living in Powers. He'd called it home for a long time now, but he occasionally wished he lived closer to Polly and Hank. Although Hank's life was wherever he was ordered to go. He couldn't give up the Brawlers Crew. Those boys were like his sons.

"Sooner than your boyfriend."

"Ouch, thanks, am I in for the cradle robber jokes?" He knew the answer, but he asked the question anyway.

"Definitely, what else did you expect?"

"True, you are your mother's son."

"As much as I'd love to stay up with you all night, I gotta crash."

"Yeah, me too. Polly doesn't give a shit if I sleep all day, but I hate to do that."

"Go curl up with your man, but keep it down."

"Nothing's going on."

"Not yet," Hank quipped as he pushed up from the chair.

Bull followed and reached out to pull his son into his arms. They hugged each other tightly without saying a word. That was more than he deserved. He'd lost himself in the oblivion of a bottle for most of Hank's life. Bull had been surly and closed off, but he'd loved Polly and their son.

"Quit with the regret bullshit, Pop. There ain't a damn thing for you to be forgiven for, so stop punishing yourself."

Bull nodded and released him, Hank turned and deftly strode across the expanse of sand toward the house. He bent to pick up the two mugs and followed. He slipped his fingers through both handles and slid the sliding door closed. The room was dark except for the hood light on the stove.

Being alone turned into his natural state over the last few years. The house was crowded and never quiet, he interacted, joked, worked, but in the end, he'd kept himself separate. Finding someone especially became something he'd avoided. That changed when a gorgeous, younger man came up to him at Brawlers and bought him a coffee.

Bull took one look at Gregory when he'd walked through the door. He'd been out of place in his designer clothes, and the look on his face showed he was ready to run. The intensity of Bull's need to claim him made turning that double down at the end of the night damn near impossible. That good-looking man not meant for him. At least that's what he kept telling himself, yet his heart wasn't listening to his head.

He rinsed the mugs and started to turn when he knew he wasn't alone.

"Thought you'd be out longer." Gregory stepped up to his side and turned to lean back against the counter.

"Hank needed rest."

"What's wrong," Gregory asked.

"What do you mean?"

"Come on, Archer." Gregory mouth tilted into a smile. "When you're thinking too much you get this little tic in your jaw right here," Gregory stroked right beneath his ear.

"I do?"

"Yeah, and you're still answering questions with questions."

"I just don't see how they forgave me for what I put them through. The drinking. The anger."

"Maybe because there's nothing to forgive you for, yes, you made mistakes out the ass. No one can deny that. But you weren't you, Bull. You cheated them out of the real Archer Woods."

"The surly asshole who busts heads for a living."

"Some of your better qualities."

"We've definitely warped your brain."

"Possibly, but I don't mind in the least. Now, it's time for you to get some rest, I know you." Gregory lifted his chin and brushed his lips to the corner of Bull's mouth. "You're going to get up early no matter how tired you are."

Bull wanted to grab the man and pull his mouth in for a real kiss. One filled with passion and lust, one which ended with Gregory under him. Each fucking second that passed, Bull found it harder to resist the lure that was Gregory Charles. He wanted the whole package, more than wanted, he needed to own Gregory. And it terrified him.

"Speaking of rest, what are you still doing up?"

"Well, I was rudely awakened by a grown ass man jumping up and down on the bed giggling like a maniacal toddler repeating Daddy."

Bull forgot it was early and everyone else was sleeping as he let out loud guffaws. Gregory's hands covered his mouth but barely muffled it. The smaller man rested his head on Bull's chest as Gregory shook with laughter.

"It wasn't that funny," An offended baritone sounded from the couch.

That just made them louder, especially when Polly and Hal yelled shut up from their bedroom upstairs. Okay, life was pretty damn good and got better with Gregory. Maybe he'd punished himself enough, and it was finally time for him to be happy with someone. He couldn't deny he needed that someone to be the man chuckling loudly in his arms.

14 BULL NEEDS TO PUT CLOTHES ON NOW!

Gregory was thankful for the sunglasses covering his eyes. He could easily glare at all the men and women thinking they could look at Bull. The man was currently playing volleyball with Polly, Hal, and Hank. His tanned skin dampened with sweat and covered in patches of sand where he'd dove for the ball.

Powerful muscles bunched and released beneath Bull's darkly tanned skin. The low-slung board shorts showed off the start of tight, dark pubic curls. What was worse, the man was smiling, and it handsomely crinkled the corners of his mismatched eyes. There was no way the man should have gotten more attractive, but the open, bright expression definitely did it.

He could see the others looking and appreciating what Gregory considered his. Gregory didn't like it. Jealousy was an emotion he'd never experienced enough to know how to handle it. He wanted to get up and walk across the sand, grab the man's rough cheeks and kiss him. Show everyone Bull was taken.

He closed his eyes and tried to focus on getting his heart rate back under control. The last two days, they'd taken him out to sightsee, and to eat. Today he'd only wanted to relax with Bull. He didn't fully understand how he'd fallen that deep so quickly. Arnold still hadn't signed the papers and made a bother of himself at Gregory's every turn. It was the single bleak spot in the last few months.

Living at the farm was amazing. He loved the guys. Finally, he felt like he had a family all his own including nieces and a nephew. In the part of his brain where he's stashed away his hopes for his life, it was exactly what he'd envisioned. And he didn't want to lose it, and he definitely didn't want to drive Bull away.

He caught Bull watching him with what could only be need. He'd analyzed it, but the conversation he'd overheard between Bull and Hank cleared everything up. Voices carried. It wasn't just Bull's age that held him back, but his temper and alcoholism.

Gregory wouldn't say it didn't bother him in some way, but Bull hadn't had a drink in ten years. Also, the man never made a move toward him in anger, if anything it was the exact opposite. Bull was always careful of him, made sure he was comfortable and happy.

But right now, he was nowhere near happy, he'd decided to wait until he got home so he could make sure Arnold signed the papers. Gregory wanted to be free of the past. His phone ringing caused him to open his eyes.

He slid his finger across the screen to answer it and pressed it to his ear, "Hello?"

"Wow, I actually hear from my son after, oh, what is it, two months?"

His mother annoyed voice made him smile.

"Who decided it was a good idea to sail around the world?"

"Don't answer a question with a question, Gregory, it's beneath you."

"Where are you," Gregory asked.

"We just docked at home. Our satellite's been a bit sketchy the last month. It definitely needs to be replaced before we do this again. I know you're busy and all, but would an email kill you?"

His parents lived on their boat and sailed around, he loved that they'd decided to do what they wanted with their lives. They'd worked jobs they'd hated and did well with investments, his dad worked as a boat mechanic when they needed money and Mom did the accounting for the Marina where they were docked. It was a semi-retirement, but they loved it, and everything could be done remotely. Which let them travel as they wanted. The owner was a bit bohemian and extremely laid back, so he wasn't strict at all.

"Sorry, it's been crazy, Mama, I left Arnold."

"Bout damn time."

"Mama."

"Don't Mama me. I told you, you shouldn't have married him. Are you okay?"

"You better not be working, baby, I'll redden—"

"Mother is on the phone."

Bull loudly laughed and fell back onto the lounger using the towel to dry himself off, and he almost forgot he was talking to his mom.

"Who's that?"

"That's Bull. He's a friend of Landon, I've been staying at his farm while I sort out the divorce."

"Bull, what kind of name is Bull."

"It correctly describes his temperament." He snorted at Bull's dirty look and yelped as he was snapped with the towel. "Don't be an asshole, Bull." It earned him an eye roll.

"Do you need to come stay with us for awhile?"

"No, I'm happy where I am, and at the moment I'm sitting on a beach in Florida taking a vacation."

"You never take vacations."

"Bull ordered me. We're visiting his ex-wife Polly who's amazing. Also, Bull's son is home on leave."

"Sounds like you're having a great time. We wanted to see about visiting."

"When?"

"I don't know since you're living at someone's farm."

"Hold on…" He turned to Bull. "My parents wanted to visit."

"If they don't mind, we could put them up in Psycho's trailer while they're visiting."

"You don't think Psycho would care? We'd have to have a family meeting with Twitch and Crave."

His mother screeched in his ear, "Psycho? Twitch and Crave?"

"I can hear her she's asking so loud."

"Sorry." Gregory smiled sadly.

"Explain to her."

"What the hell is going on, Gregory?"

"Um, I live with Bull, but also Crave and Twitch, they're married, and a sweetheart named Hunter. He's quiet, but once he gets comfortable, he's friendly. They're security and bartenders at a biker bar called Brawlers. So, you'd have to be quiet while they sleep during the day. Psycho who lives with his husband in a cottage close by has a trailer we're sure he wouldn't mind you using. It's behind the barn and Bull's workshop."

"You're living with bikers?"

"Yes, but they're sweet as can be, well, you'll have to watch Bull he's a bit surly."

"Oh, I'm so happy, you finally got the stick removed from your ass, was the surgery expensive?"

Bull snorted not even pretending he wasn't listening in.

"Your sense of humor hasn't improved in the last few months."

"Just because you can't appreciate my humor than I raised you wrong."

"If I remember correctly, I was forbidden from anything that would interfere with my studies."

"If you were normal you would've rebelled like any self-respecting teenager."

"You're all heart, Mama. So, when can we expect you?"

"Hold on…" He heard silence then his mother hollering, "Marty, our son is living with a biker gang, we gotta go visit."

"Aggie, have you been drinking again?" His father thick southern drawl came through loud and clear.

"Yes, but that's got nothing to do with this. When do you want to go?"

Bull was losing it beside him, and he leaned sideways to slap his chest which only made the man laugh louder.

"I gotta finish two more engines, probably be about a week."

"Hear that, Gregory?"

"Yeah, that'd be perfect. We're in Florida for another four days, and then we fly back. I work from home so anytime after that."

"Tell them we'll pick them up at the airport."

"Bull said—"

"I heard him, sweetie, that's one sexy drawl. Just something about them slow talking country boys ain't there?"

He couldn't help chuckling as she changed her usual flat accent to a strong southern one. No one would ever know the woman was from New York. The only family left there was his cousin, Gideon. Really other than his parents, Gideon was it. He should call him and check in, it had been awhile.

"I don't know what you mean."

"Whatever, give us seven days to make arrangements, and I'll let you know what time to be at the airport. Your father is shirtless and covered in grease, it's distracting me, so I gotta go."

He shook his head. "Okay, love you, Mama."

"Love you too."

He disconnected the call. His parents had in some ways disillusioned him. He'd wanted that. High school sweethearts, teenage parents, shitty jobs and even shittier places to live, they'd unconditionally loved each other through it all.

"Um, interesting parents."

"Yes, they are, but other than the Twirled Crews and the Brawler couples I've never seen anyone so much in love. When I started dating, and I realized my parents were the exception. By all accounts, their lives could've been miserable, but they loved unconditionally."

116

"Probably a letdown when you've had nothing to live up to it."

"Exactly, are you sure you want—"

"It sounds like you haven't seen them in a while. It'll be good for you. Although you're right, we're going to have to talk to Crave and Twitch, also Psycho and Ben, those two like having sex outside way too much."

"It wouldn't be so bad if it wasn't broad daylight."

"True, we'll see if we can keep them to outside sex only during nighttime."

"It would be appreciated. But they didn't start embarrassing me until I moved out, then it was as if they reverted to teenagers again."

"It's gotta be hard to get married and have a family when you're still kids."

Gregory liked Bull remembered even the smallest details of what Gregory told him. It made him feel as if he was important to Bull. And after the other night, he knew he was at least enough for now. They've only been friends for months, they hadn't even had a date—oh shit, they did have a date. The ride and dinner, that constituted a date, right?

"It was. They struggled constantly, but they never let it get them down."

"Marks of a healthy relationship."

"I think so. Did you win?"

"No, Hal and I let Polly and Hank win."

"Sure. You and Hal getting a bit out of shape?"

"I'll have you know I'm in perfect shape for a man half my age."

Gregory scanned Bull from head to toe, he had to admit it was true. Bull boxed three times a week, worked out at least a couple, handled custom jobs in his workshop and kept rowdy crowds under control. Except for his occasional cigar and his penchant for coffee that could strip paint the man took care of himself. Even if the man had a belly, he'd still want him.

Everything about Bull did it for him. His dominance, protectiveness, and the love he had for those he considered his. The Brawler Crew were like his sons. He was a pushover for his nieces and nephew.

"You're alright."

"Alright, I'll show you alright, baby," Bull shouted and surged to his feet.

Before he had a chance to protest he was tossed over Bull's shoulder. He was jostled as Bull easily jogged toward the water. Gregory didn't have an opportunity to brace himself, and he found himself dunked into cold water. He surfaced to find Bull smiling at him, his eyes twinkling with happiness. There was no way he could ever describe how much he loved that.

"You're an asshole!" Gregory placed his hands on Bull's shoulders and pushed him under.

Bull broke the surface laughing and sputtering.

"The water is fucking freezing," Gregory whined.

"Aw, poor baby," Bull crooned and embraced Gregory.

Bull was warm even with the cold water surrounding them. He laid his head on Bull's shoulder as they tread water. They didn't talk and didn't have to, it was nice just to be silent with someone. Yes, they talked a lot, but sometimes they could just sit there and be content.

Freezing or not, Gregory didn't want to give this up. He just wanted a little more time to savor it. Gregory felt he couldn't move forward with Bull or even try until he got Arnold to agree to the divorce. A fresh start, that's all he wanted, and he needed it to start with the gorgeous man who'd done nothing but protect and make him happy. Four more days and he could put his quickly forming plan into motion, yet for now, he was satisfied with this.

15 RESISTANCE WAS NO LONGER AN OPTION

The week ended too quickly, Bull loved having Gregory pretty much to himself, but it was back to Powers. Gregory had a ton of work to catch up on and hadn't worked from home as much. Hell, the man was already in bed by the time Bull got home from Brawlers. No more watching the sunrise before bed. Fuck, when had it happened. His resistance fled, and all that remained was a need he barely controlled.

It was worse than any craving he'd ever had for a drink. The past two nights Bull barely looked at the bourbon before he stood and headed home.

He roughly pushed his fingers through his hair. Lights were on inside. He dismounted from his bike and quickly strode across the yard to the back door. Bull pulled open the door to the scents of coffee and dinner. The bluesy music played loudly. He caught the screen door and eased it shut.

Gregory stood at the stove with his back to him. Pajama bottoms hung low on slim hips, and Bull's lips quirked at the edges seeing Gregory in one of his shirts. The man had started to take a page out of Twitch's book. Twitch stole shirts from Crave over the years because he wanted something of the big man's.

Gregory bent over to check something in the oven. Bull groaned, and thankfully the music drowned out the sound. His cock hardened and he stepped forward, quickly closing the distance between them. The man straightened and Bull pushed up behind him. He didn't even try to hide the hard ridge of his dick.

"Bull, you're home…" Gregory jerked against him. "Early."

"What'cha making," Bull asked as he gripped Gregory's hips and tugged the man's ass tight to him.

"Just, um, I threw in," Gregory cleared his throat, "one of the casseroles Twitch made."

Gregory's head fell back onto Bull's shoulder. He slipped his hands beneath Gregory's shirt and smoothed his rough palms over Gregory's taut stomach, then up to Gregory's chest. He pinched the man's pebbled nipples. Fuck, Gregory whimpered so sweetly for him.

He placed a soft kiss beneath Gregory's ear. "Ya want it don't ya, boy?"

Gregory nodded.

"Turn off the stove and oven."

Gregory obeyed without question. He turned the younger man around and lowered his head until his mouth barely touched Gregory's soft lips.

"That's my boy. You're going to go to my room and wait for me, understand?"

Gregory was practically vibrating in his arms with his harsh, labored breathing. Gregory's voice shook as he answered yes.

"You have ten minutes to make a decision, you tell me yes or no. If you say yes, there's no going back. Tell me you know what that means."

"Yes, you'll own me."

"Every inch of you, your pleasure and pain, every time you cum it's only for me."

Gregory sagged against him.

"Go, I'll be up in a few minutes." Bull retreated and put a safe distance between them. Gregory watched him for a few moments before he turned and disappeared out of the kitchen.

The decision to give Gregory a chance to think was probably stupid on his part. He fucking needed the answer to be yes, but what he required was Gregory's trust. Bull craved Gregory's submission. If that was even possible with Gregory's past, remained to be seen.

He quickly wrote a note that dinner was in the oven, then turned off all the lights. Bull walked to the fridge, opened it to grab a couple bottles of water. He had no intention of letting Gregory out of his bed anytime soon, if ever.

He took the steps two at a time, then walked down the long hallway to his room at the end. The door was open, and his bedside lamp dimly illuminated the interior. He slowed his pace and took a deep breath.

Once inside his room, he kicked his door closed and turned his head to find Gregory stiffly perched on the end of his big bed. He didn't say anything just walked to his dresser and set the bottles down, he took a look in the mirror. Studying the lines on his face and the shocking silver in his hair and beard.

Shit, what the fuck am I doing, Bull asked himself.

He had thought about making Gregory his for months. He wouldn't fuck it up because he had waited too long.

Slowly he turned to face Gregory and found the man watching him. He lifted his arms and reached back to grab the back of his shirt, tugged it over his head. He bent over to unlace his boots, removed them and his socks. As he stood up, he locked his gaze on Gregory's. Gregory wasn't hardened or adept at hiding his emotions, the man's eyes gave everything away. At that moment, Gregory was nervous, maybe a little scared. He didn't want that.

"Gregory."

"Yes."

"Do you know what I thought the first time I saw you," he asked.

"That I was a pain in the ass boy."

He felt a smile tug at the corner of his mouth. "No, I hated that fucking ring. You're still wearing it."

"It's habit."

Gregory dropped his gaze to his hand and nervously toyed with the gold band.

He closed the distance between them. No more fucking around. No more second guessing. It was time he staked his claim. He held out his hand for Gregory's and waited for the other man to reach out. Seconds past but it felt like a lifetime before Gregory placed his soft, slender hand in his.

Bull placed his thumb and index finger on the body warmed metal.

"Gregory, this is where you tell me yes or no. Baby, we can stop now, you can go to your room, and tomorrow will be a new day. Nothing changes. But before you answer, I want to explain something."

"Okay."

"Being mine means I'll never put my hands on you in anger. You're a grown man, and I'll never criticize you or your decisions. I won't make promises that I won't tip over the edge and never drink again. I don't know all that flowery shit people like to hear. We've danced around this for months, now all I need to know is, yes or no?"

He was prepared to wait as long as Gregory needed. The man's past would be a huge roadblock. He just held onto the ring and wanted it off, it was the first step, and Gregory had to take the leap of faith.

Gregory's wavy hair fell to conceal his beautiful face as the man studied the ring. He sensed the hesitation, but he refused to retreat.

"Yes."

The single word was spoken so softly he had barely heard it. He raised his right hand to circle Gregory's slender wrist and slowly slid the ring off. The tension in his man eased as soon as the metal slipped free. He tucked it into his pocket when he'd rather toss it in the nearest wastebasket.

He released Gregory, then placed his palms on the man's cheeks. Gregory's skin was soft and warm, and he used his thumbs to tip Gregory's head back. His bed was high off the ground, so he didn't have to lean too far until he allowed his mouth to hover above the younger man's full lips.

"So beautiful." He bumped his nose to Gregory's and as the man advanced he retreated. Gregory whined. "Love that sound. Stand up," he ordered.

He straightened and stepped back, Gregory eased off the bed. His man looked so nervous, almost innocent.

"I see you like my clothes."

"It was comfortable and possibly made it into my laundry."

"As much as I like you in my clothes, take two steps forward and strip."

His cock filled and pushed against the back of his zipper. Gregory looked away.

"No, look at me the whole time. The only time you're allowed to look away is when you take off my shirt. Now, strip."

He was dominant, wouldn't deny it, but he wasn't someone's Sir or Master. He just liked control. It was his job to make sure his man got off. He liked rough, yet that wasn't what he had in mind for Gregory. His shy and insecure man probably had a million ideas going through his head, but Bull was sure none of them matched what he had planned.

Gregory obeyed perfectly. Only broke eye contact when the shirt slipped over his head. Lightly tanned skin stretched over lean muscle. Gregory had the sexiest little paunch to his stomach. Pale, cinnamon freckles dusted Gregory's chest and shoulders. He wanted to kiss every one of them, but first, he had to get his man ready.

"Keep going."

He didn't miss the breath Gregory took before shaking hands pushed at the waistband of the pajama bottoms Gregory wore.

Fuck, neatly trimmed curls surrounded the base of the prettiest dick Bull had ever seen. Gregory's nervousness was getting the better of him, he sensed it. At last, Gregory kicked the pants aside. Fine, light brown hair dusted Gregory's slender legs.

"No," Bull growled as Gregory tried to cover himself. That wouldn't do. "What do you like?"

"Like?"

"How do you liked to be touched?"

"I don't know."

Gregory appeared saddened by that answer as if the man really didn't know his own wants and needs.

"I like when you touch me," Gregory whispered, dropped his gaze to the floor.

He allowed the man to look away and stepped closer, savored the warmth of his man. Raising his hand, he threaded his fingers through Gregory's silky hair. Tightening his grip, he jerked the man's head back until Gregory looked at him.

Slowly he lowered his mouth to Gregory's, "I've thought about this since the moment you walked into Brawlers."

He didn't slam his mouth roughly onto Gregory's. He took his time, gently nipping and brushing the full curves of the man's lips. The touch of Gregory's hands was hesitant as they settled on his sides. He sensed Gregory hadn't received the gentlest treatment, but he was determined to change that. With a subtle pressure from his grip on Gregory's hair, he urged the man to tilt his head.

Gregory's quickened, uneven breaths fanned his mouth, and he parted his lips to flick Gregory's top lip, then slipped inside. He teased Gregory until Gregory relaxed, the man's smooth skin pressed against his hairy chest. Gregory shivered at the contact. He slightly bent his knees and wrapped his right arm around Gregory's lean frame and lifted him.

The bed was only a few short steps away, and he laid them down without removing his mouth from Gregory's. He easily positioned Gregory high on the bed with Gregory's head on his pillow. Breaking the kiss, he straightened and sat back on his heels.

His man vibrated with nervousness, and he was a bastard for finding it sexy. Even at Gregory's age and experience, the was still unsure, but not for long. Bull planned to love him until Gregory could think of nothing else but him.

16 GREGORY WAS TERRIFIED

Gregory felt like he was coming out of his skin. His heart was beating so frantically he swore the bed shook with the force. He was terrified. His sexual experiences were lukewarm at best. The last few times with Arnold, those he wanted to forget. What if he disappointed Bull?

He stared up at Bull. The man's silver hair with the slight wave fell around Bull's face, and Bull watched him from under heavy lids. Bull's powerful chest expanded with his sharp inhalations. He was gorgeous, and Gregory felt unattractive beside him. He wanted to suck in the roundness of his stomach. Hide from Bull's heated gaze, but he was powerless to move.

Bull loomed over him, moved his mismatched gaze over Gregory, and he fisted his fingers in the quilt beside his hips. Being naked in front of Bull was strangely erotic with Bull still half dressed.

Bull made a sudden move to the side, and he didn't hide his flinch in time. His face flushed with shame.

"Gregory, what did I say earlier?" Bull asked calmly.

"That you'd never put your hands on me in anger."

"And I won't."

"I know, I just—"

"It's okay. No need to explain."

Bull's voice was soft, caring, he closed his eyes to calm himself. He tracked Bull's movements, listened to the glide of the nightstand drawer, and then the bed shifted.

"Open your eyes."

He obeyed to find Bull setting a bottle of lube and a condom on the bed.

"Nothing has to happen, fuck knows I want to feel your ass around my cock, but that isn't what this about. If it happens, it does, if not, we have all the time in the world. I just want to feel you. Make you feel good."

Calloused hands gripped his hips, thumbs teased the edge of his pubes, and it began. Bull massaged his side and stomach, up and down, teased his hardened nipples. His breath caught at the back of his throat. It was gentle and slow as if Bull really believed there wasn't a reason to rush.

"S'beautiful and sexy."

Gregory opened his mouth to protest but ceased when Bull pulled back. He dropped his gaze to watch Bull work his belt loose, then popped the button on his jeans. He held his breath as Bull eased the zipper of his jeans down. A thick, dark bush with a liberal peppering of silver almost had him reaching out. He stayed still, though, he wanted to see it all. He'd imaged this moment since the day Bull almost flashed his dick when Twitch's condom and lube prank went wrong.

Fuck, Bull pushed up and shoved the denim off his hips. The peek of the thick, dusky base gave way to expose a wide, veined shaft. It wasn't monstrous in length, but in width, shit, that was going to hurt. He whimpered and tried to get away when the uncut head with the thick gauge ring placed vertically through the tip appeared. He whimpered and started to scoot backward.

Bull's strong arms wrapped around his thighs and tugged him back into place.

"Where do you think you're going?"

"Um, that's as big around—"

Bull chuckled darkly and lowered onto his body. The hardness of Bull's cock sunk into the softness of his stomach. The body warmed metal of his piercing felt off but arousing. Bull's forearms rested beside his head and rough fingertips caught in his hair.

"You'll love it."

"Arrogance."

As he said it, his nervousness eased, and his cock started to harden at the sensation of Bull's hairy belly tickling his cock.

"Confidence, I know what my boy needs."

He raised his hands to thread his fingers through the hair on Bull's stomach and stroked upward until he wrapped his arms around Bull's neck.

"I'm not a boy."

"Compared me you are."

"Do you have an issue with our ages?"

Bull kissed him softly, once, twice, "I did, maybe I still do." A third kiss longer and a bit rougher stroked over his lips. "But I've denied this as long as I could. You've been in my house for months. Teasing me just by being in the same room. Sleeping a few doors down. Fuck, jerking off didn't even take the edge off."

"You—"

"Since the night I fucking met you. I came home that night. I needed to know what you looked like naked and in my bed. It pissed me off you belonged to someone else."

"I thought you couldn't stand me."

"I wanted you more than I wanted that drink I was staring into."

He moaned as Bull rocked against his stomach. He traced the tattooed patterns on Bull's arms and shoulders. Teased the faint dusting on hairs on Bull's shoulders. Everything about Bull turned him on, from his grumpy nature to his hairy body. As much as he wanted to have sex with Bull, all the times he thought about it, he was content to just be there. Bull's massive body on top of his as they talked.

"You can have me."

"For how long?"

"What do you mean?"

There was a hint of insecurity in Bull's eyes. The vulnerability took him aback.

"I want this to be more than a fuck, I need it to be more. I've waited so fucking long. Will you give me a chance?"

"Like partners chance?"

"Exactly."

"Yes."

Before the word was completely out of his mouth Bull's lips were on his and Bull rolled onto his back taking him with him.

"Take off my jeans."

He nodded and scooted down, he curled his fingers in the soft fabric and tugged them down Bull's thick thighs and muscular calves. He loved every inch of Bull.

"Bull," he said as he removed Bull's jeans and dropped them over the side of the bed.

"No, say my name."

A smile tugged at the corner of his mouth. "Archer."

"That's better, now, come here."

He crawled back up Bull's body. He laid on top of Bull, and the kisses began, soft and gentle. One after another, no words were spoken. The only sounds in the room a cacophony of moans and groans hitched breaths.

Then an unmanly squeak as Bull pushed his slicked fingers to his hole. He clenched. He was embarrassed and hid his face, only a few hours ago he'd laid in bed fucking himself with his favorite toy along to a fantasy of Bull taking him.

"No, no hiding from me. S'good."

A single, thick finger breached him, and he pushed back against it. Bull's free hand were again in his hair. Kisses brushed his face, his mouth, and along his throat as Bull slowly stretched him. Bull's pre-come hot and wet against his stomach. Bull pushed a second, then a third and Gregory whimpered and begged like a slut as he rode Bull's fingers with languid arches and rotations of his hips.

The air conditioning kicking on cooled the sweat on his skin, goosebumps pebbled his skin. Bull whispered dirty, sweet promises between kisses that turned gentle and rough with dizzying speeds, only to turn tender again. The backs of Bull's fingers brushed his prostate repeatedly, that and his rutting against the solid curve of Bull's stomach had him so close.

"Bu…"

Bull growled.

"Archer, I'm gonna…"

His balls drew up tight, and his cock pulsed a painful rhythm as he pushed down onto Bull's stomach. He rubbed harder and screamed as four fingers stretched him until his pleasure bordered on agony.

"Come for me, baby," Bull growled beside his ear.

He arched and humped as Bull finger fucked him until the man's hand slapped against his ass. He dropped his head and bit down on Bull's chest, screaming around the flesh in his mouth. Nothing had ever come close to that. It was soft and gentle but so intense his head swam. He wanted more, hell, he needed more. His orgasm hadn't even taken the edge off. Archer inside him, fucking him into the mattress was what he craved.

Bull rolled them, he felt empty without Bull's fingers inside him. He attempted to hold tight to Bull, but the man pulled away, the tearing of a condom wrapper and the snick of the lube cap filled the room.

He looked up to find Bull's face flushed and his features tight. The big man's hands shook. That barely restrained need was for him. He'd done that to a man like Bull. He reached out and pushed Bull's hands aside, he finished rolling the latex down Bull's length. Every jerk and moan, he savored it all.

Once the barrier was in place, Bull laid on him and reached between their bodies. He felt the thick ring first, and he automatically pushed out, and they groaned in unison as Bull slowly slid inside.

"S'fucking perfect."

Bull's words were a warm rush against his mouth. He wrapped his legs around Bull, hooked his feet over his thighs, and sighed at the incredible way Bull and he fit. He didn't have long to ponder or analyze what it meant. Bull began a slow and gentle rhythm.

Their bodies came together, dance as seamless as the one they'd shared in the kitchen. He inhaled the scents of sex, sweat, and the subtle hint of Bull's soap. His eyes burned at the tender kisses. The sweet words. Even though there wasn't an inch of space between their frames, he clutched Bull closer.

Bull's lips brushed his on every retreat and thrust.

"Need you so much. So long. Dreamed of you in my bed."

"Archer."

He cried out as the fat, pierced head of Bull's cock tortured his gland in a lazy pace.

"Say it again."

"Archer."

"Again."

Each time he called Bull's real name the snap of Bull's hips increased. He felt another orgasm building, and he forced his thighs wider and canted his hips. His eyes rolled back in his head. No one had ever loved him, plenty had fucked him, but this, this with Bull was something else. He wanted his man to lose it, to come deep inside him, yet he also didn't want it to end.

"Come on, baby, I know you want to. Come around my cock. Do it."

Bull's teeth pinched his earlobe, and the slam of the other man's hips became almost painful. Piston hard snap, pause and repeat. He dug his short nails into the tensed upward arch of Bull's back. He dropped his feet flat to the mattress, threw his head back and screamed Bull's name. Seed splattered his belly, and Bull froze above him.

Bull rolled his hips, grinding through his orgasm. He was so stretched around Bull's cock he felt each pulse. Relished the sound of his name repeated in Bull's gravelly voice. Bull collapsed on top of him, and he automatically wrapped his arms and legs around him. He wasn't ready to let him go. Wasn't willing to feel empty again.

They shared one more lingering kiss and Bull laid his forehead on his.

He stroked his hands lazily over Bull's slick back. Turning his head, he kissed Bull's shoulder, licked at the mark he'd left.

"You okay," Bull asked.

"Perfect, but I think I need a shower."

"You and me both, want to share?"

"Yes."

He loathed the emptiness but savored the soreness as Bull reached between them again to hold onto the condom and slip free. The big man rolled from the bed, disposed of the condom, then Bull held out his hand. He took it and let his man help him off the bed. His legs shook, and his thighs ached, but he'd never felt better.

Before Bull led him from the room, Bull kissed him again. He could get used to being Bull's and hoped he never had to go back to the before. Being there, he was happy, and he wanted to stay that way.

17 SOME PEOPLE HAD MORE BALLS THAN BRAINS

The incessant ring of the doorbell pulled him from sleep, and he looked over Gregory's head to check the time. "Motherfuckers, it's not even fucking noon yet," Bull bellowed as he rolled from bed and the warm, gorgeous man beside him. He didn't bother getting dressed. People would fucking learn not to come by his place before noon.

It should be a capital offense.

"Bull, where are you going," Gregory asked sleepily.

"Someone wants to die."

"Are Crave and Twitch at it again?"

"No, someone's at the door."

He muttered as he exited his room and made his way downstairs toward the door. His fingers had just wrapped around the door knob, turned it when he heard Gregory calling his name.

"What," he asked jerking the door open.

A couple about his age stood on his porch. Both of them stared right at his cock. A sheet appeared out of nowhere and blocked his lower body from sight.

"What the fuck do y'all—"

"Mom, Dad, you're early, I told you three."

Shit, a great way to meet the parents. He let his head fall back and realized Gregory was just as naked as him. No time for a hard-on or to carry his man back to bed.

Parents, Bull, your man's parents, you can behave, even his inner voice didn't sound confident.

"Our plane got in early." It was all Gregory's dad said.

The man was shorter than him and not as broad. He didn't see much of Gregory in him, but the woman, Gregory took after his mom. Same bright green eyes and impish smile.

"Son, should we let you have a few more minutes or an hour?"

Gregory's mother sounded more amused than scandalized. He liked her already.

"Mom, behave, just because you've gone all bohemian in your retired life, it's still weird."

"Fine. Do we get introduced? In my day, a lady got the name of a man before she saw his—"

"Mom."

He chuckled and held out his hand. "Name's Bull."

Gregory's dad shook it a bit reluctantly, but his mom grabbed his hand and held on.

"Bull, such a pleasure to meet you. I'm Aggie, and this is Marty. I'm sort of a hugger, but we'll save that for when you're dressed."

"Understandable. Come on in."

He and Gregory stepped back in tandem. Gregory held the sheet around them.

"Is it a raid?"

Crave's voice came from behind him, and he turned to find Crave hanging half out his door. Twitch peeked around his bicep. Hunter was staying back and sneaking a glance from just inside the hallway.

"Gregory's parents are here. Temp, new rules in place."

"Yes, Daddy, we'll make a great impression on the in-laws."

"Crave, I fucking swear I may not evict you, but I will kick your ass."

"Whatever, old man."

"Archer, no bloodshed," Gregory ordered.

"Fine."

"Thank you."

"Kitchen is through there. We're going to go get dressed."

"I made cinnamon rolls, coffee cake, oatmeal bars, and fruit salad last night."

He looked at Twitch in time to see the man's cheeks turn pink.

"I was nervous about meeting them, leave me alone."

The little man disappeared into the room, seconds later Crave slammed the door.

"New people make Twitch a bit nervous. It's fine," Gregory said fondly.

"Where's Psycho and Ben? I believe you said, we'll be using his trailer."

"Oh, they live in the cottage on the other side of the fence with Psycho's ex-wife Bernie and her wife, Stacey. It's a long story. You'll meet them later for breakfast."

Nothing much made him uncomfortable, but the longer he stood with Gregory hidden behind him and wrapped in one sheet it was getting weird. He also noticed Gregory's dad hadn't said a word except to say their plane landed early.

"Breakfast, it's already the afternoon," Aggie asked.

"Our schedule is a little weird."

"We're going to get dressed, now."

Bull bent his knees and picked Gregory up to carry him piggyback to the bedroom.

"I think we flashed ass at my parents."

Gregory laughed as he dropped the man on the bed.

"Why wasn't I warned about parents?"

"I did, you remember I texted you last Friday to say they were coming but would rent a car because they didn't know when their flight would land."

"No, I don't remember, and if—"

"Quit being an asshole. If you put on pants to answer the door like a normal person, this wouldn't have happened."

"When have we ever been normal in this house?"

Gregory seemed to take a minute to consider it, "True, very, very true."

"And I haven't met parents since Polly's, and I was probably five, they knew me my whole life."

Gregory sat up and held out his arms. He stepped into them and leaned down to kiss Gregory's soft hair.

"We don't have to tell them—"

Which was exceptionally stupid because it wasn't like him and Gregory didn't share a sheet naked to greet them.

"That's not what I want, and you fucking know it."

"I didn't say it was."

"Do you want to keep it secret?"

Even though he hoped the answer would be no but prepared for the yes. As much as he wanted one night to change everything, he knew Gregory was still married and the last five years were hell for Gregory. It was way too early to hope for more.

"No." Gregory placed a kiss on his stomach. "Like you said last night, we've been dancing around this for months. I think everyone knew before us."

He combed his fingers through Gregory's hair. "Oh, I knew, I just fought it."

"No more, okay?"

"Okay. Let's get dressed before the Brawlers descend on them."

"Good idea, hopefully, one of our kids behaves."

He growled as Gregory bounced off the bed to head to his own room. They'd have to remedy that soon.

"Don't start adopting."

"Too late."

He started after Gregory but reminded himself he needed to get dressed. He was too old for this shit.

■■■■

"Touch my motherfucking stomach one more time, Psycho, and I will fucking castrate you," Stacey's voice was the only warning he'd got before she was busting into the room with Psycho on her heels.

A few weeks before the twins moved for the first time and Psycho was obsessed with not missing a kick. It was also making the usually even-tempered Stacy insane.

"Psy, please, leave Stacey alone."

"But, baby, what if—"

"We've discussed this, we've allowed you an hour each day to cuddle with the belly."

"Yes, dear."

Bull snorted before taking a big swallow of his coffee and watched Psycho pout. If the man wasn't crazy, they would give him shit about it more. Bernie and Stacey spent two years trying to talk Psycho into donating, it wasn't until Ben came into the picture that Psycho relented. Since then, the huge man was obsessed with every phase of Stacey's pregnancy, every ache or pain, any sign of exhaustion, Psycho tried to drag her to the doctor.

Instead of a simple donation for Bernie and Stacey to have a family. Ben had thrown in a stipulation that he'd only agree if they moved to town. They'd co-parent any children they'd have together. It was an odd arrangement, but nothing was normal around the farm.

He glanced at Aggie and Marty to find them watching the new arrivals with amusement. He introduced Gregory's parents to Psycho, Ben, Stacey, and Bernie. The conversation easily flowed around him, but he remained silent and took it in.

He reached out and rested his arm along the back of Gregory's chair, he gently drew circles on Gregory's arm with his thumb. Over the months, his need to touch Gregory intensified to an almost obsessiveness level, but since he'd had Gregory in his bed—taken his body and claimed him, he didn't want the man away from him.

Gregory turned to give him a small smile before turning back to his breakfast.

"Bull," Aggie said his name. "Gregory tells me you have a son."

"Yes, Hank, he's in the Marines."

"You must be very proud."

"I am. He followed in my footsteps. I would've chosen a different life for him, but he does what makes him happy."

"How did you meet my son," Marty finally opened his mouth.

"He came into Brawlers one night for Landon and Zerk's anniversary party."

He was trying not to point out in his usual asshole fashion he was older than Marty. Older than his boyfriend/partner's parent probably wasn't good idea to bring up when he was in the process of being interrogated.

"You knew he was married, right?"

"Dad."

"Baby, it's fine," he whispered. "The ring on his finger was kinda obvious."

"But you still moved him into your house. What about his husband?"

Gregory stiffened beside him. His man was keeping secrets.

"My reasons are for Gregory explain to you, but that fucker is his soon-to-be ex-husband. Gregory's mine."

Gregory's hand tentatively came to rest on his thigh. He set his mug aside and reached across his lap to lace their fingers together. At fifty-six he hadn't pictured himself meeting parents again, hell, he had reached the point he would be alone except for the crew and their partners and kids.

"I gotta go get ready for work, you okay?"

"Yes, I'm fine."

He leaned to the side and gave Gregory a quick kiss.

"Sorry, we have to cut this short, but Twitch and Gregory will be around if you need anything. Make yourself at home."

"Thank you, Bull, it was a pleasure to meet you."

He smiled at Aggie. Marty remained silent. He had a feeling it was going to take some time to win over Gregory's dad but, to be honest, he didn't care if the man liked him or not. Gregory was his, and he wasn't giving him up. He reached out and grabbed his mug, brought it to his mouth and drained it.

He stood and went to his room to get ready for the night. Unlike other nights where he dreaded coming home to his empty bed, he knew Gregory would be there waiting. Finally, something to look forward to after years of waiting.

18 IT WAS ALL SO WEIRD

Gregory stared into his mother's tear-filled eyes and then at the barely restrained rage in his father's. He hadn't wanted to go into the details of why he'd left Arnold or more correctly was rescued from his husband.

"Why didn't you tell us, Gregory, why?"

"I was embarrassed. I thought I could deal with it on my own and I thought about leaving so many times."

"You could've come home. We would've made room for you on the boat. It wouldn't have been ideal, but you would've been safe."

"I know, I know, but I'm a grown man I should've been able to handle this on my own."

"Instead, Landon called in Bull," his dad said.

The quietness and evenness of his dad's voice made him squirm in his chair. If he could have disappeared at that moment, he would have. He watched as his mom reached out and took his dad's hand.

"We're not blaming you. That's not our intention, but we didn't raise you to take shit like that."

Aside from Landon's parents, and also Lucky's, his parents were the most loving couple he knew. They'd rarely been apart a day since they'd started dating. Even thirty-seven years later, they took every opportunity to touch, to say I love you. That was always what he'd secretly wanted. That seemingly unattainable love and he hadn't found that until—shit, he wouldn't go there. It was too soon.

"Landon got concerned when he didn't hear from me and took it upon himself to call Bull."

"I'm glad he did."

"Son, is Arnold still giving you problems?"

"Yes, he calls, comes by the office, sometimes I turn around at the store, and he's there."

"Have you told Bull?"

"Yes, but not everything. Bull can be a bit…volatile."

His mother snorted and made him smile.

"That's one word for it. He's awful grumpy, honey."

"One of his more charming qualities."

"Must be—"

"Definitely love, those two have been dancing around each other for months," Twitch piped up from his position at the sink.

"Don't start, Twitch."

"Yes, Dad."

"Pain in the ass."

"Don't start sounding like Bull."

"I'm not that cranky."

"Thank fuck for that. One of our Dads has to be sensible."

"I didn't adopt y'all."

"Oh, you so did, once you hooked up with the resident Papa Bear, you got kids. But just think about it, at least we're potty trained, grown, and relatively self-sufficient."

"I'm moving back to town," he mumbled.

As soon as the words were out of his mouth, skinny arms wrapped around his neck from behind. Twitch's cute face buried against the side of his throat.

"No, please," Twitch whined. "I don't want to live in a broken home."

He laughed, raised his arm and reached back to stroke Twitch's silky hair. Twitch loved hugs and affection of any kind. The young man hadn't had any of that growing up, so he noticed the Twirled and Brawler Crews gave it freely, he'd quickly followed suit.

"I wouldn't leave you, I promise. Don't you have an appointment with Trouble?"

"Shit, forgot, lip piercing day," Twitch squealed and pulled away to bounce out of the room. The small man yelled an I love you.

"I like your new family."

"I do too. Did y'all want to go into town? Psycho's husband has this amazing bakery. He has a whole line of espresso pastries. The man is a genius."

"That sounds great, just let me go grab my purse."

His mother stood and exited the room, but his dad remained behind. His dad leaned forward to rest his arms on the table and nudged his mug out of the way.

"Son," his dad sounded hesitant. "Listen, I ain't gonna say I understand you dating a man older than me."

"If you and Mom hadn't started early, Bull wouldn't be older."

"Yeah, besides the damn point. I'm just saying it's weird. I gotta say though, you seemed to have done good this time around. You know I made it no secret I didn't like Arnold, and I'm not sorry to see you away from him. I just wished you had been honest with us. You shouldn't have put up with that shit. I wanted you to have what Aggie and I have. It's never been easy, but nothing worth having is."

"I know that, and that's what I wanted, but I felt trapped. I knew I shouldn't have said yes and I did it anyway. But, Dad, Bull's great. He treats me great. He's amazing even if grumpy. It's new. I really want this to work."

"I can tell. You did good is all I'm saying."

"Thanks."

"You're welcome. I'm gonna go see if your mom is ready."

"I'll meet you at the truck."

"Truck, son, no more foreign, high-priced vehicles, about damn time."

"I prefer Bull's bike, but he's seen me drive and won't teach me to ride."

"Smart, smart man."

He grinned at his dad's smirk and waited until he was alone to relax into his chair.

His life changed so much since he'd walked into Brawlers and he couldn't regret it, but if he could just get Arnold to sign the papers. He wanted to be free of the man. All he needed was to move on and make a life with his grumpy bear without the dark cloud of his ex threatening to ruin it. Soon, he just needed to figure out how.

■■■■

Gregory chuckled to himself as he climbed into Bull's big bed. He'd spent most of the day with his parents. They even planned to go to Brawlers the next night. He couldn't wait to see his parents in their first gay bar experience, especially when it was Brawlers.

The rumble of motorcycles caused his smile to widen. Bull texted twenty minutes ago he was headed home. It was a couple type thing, but it wasn't a new development. Rarely did he not receive a text throughout the evening. He hadn't really thought much about it. The Crews had a tendency to keep in touch. Not much went on that they didn't all know about. He'd quickly been added to the circle.

He hadn't realized how much he loved it or maybe hadn't wanted to admit it in case it turned out to be temporary.

He heard the door slam but not much other than that. The guys were quiet for once. The window-rattling music didn't start as soon as one of them could get to the stereo system. He found it weird that they couldn't handle quiet after being in a loud bar all night.

Heavy boots on hardwood sounded as Bull made his way up the steps. It had to be him since he and Bull were the only ones with rooms upstairs.

Suddenly he was nervous about what Bull would think about him being in his bed. They hadn't discussed him being there when Bull got home.

"Glad I didn't have to carry you from your bed."

"Hello to you too."

"Hey," Bull rumbled.

Bull crossed the room to lean over him and kiss him. He wrinkled his nose at the stench of stale beer.

"Did you bathe in beer tonight?"

"Jealous boyfriend, a thrown drink and a broken bottle."

"You okay?"

"I'm free of any new scars."

"I don't care about the scars, they're sexy on you." He brushed his lips across the one that slashed across Bull's cheek. It was faded with age but still noticeable.

"I'm going to shower work off me and be right back."

"Okay, did you need dinner?"

"Naw, Elijah brought in pizza on his way home earlier."

He knew they had a small kitchen at Brawlers, but it went relatively unused unless Hunter threw in a collection of fried food in the deep fryer if people actually wanted it. Elijah mentioned getting in a regular cook. It seemed a waste when most ate before they came and were happy to just drink.

He received one more kiss and Bull headed out of the room toward the bathroom. He reached for his book to kill the time it took Bull to take his shower. He wasn't really into the book and was just starting chapter three when Bull entered the room.

Bull had a towel tied low on his hips and was drying his hair with another. Damn, the man was sexy, and all his. He slowly set his book aside without taking his eyes off Bull.

Bull turned to look at him as he tossed the towel toward the hamper. He licked his lips and his stomach clenched at the look Bull was giving him. Bull slowly removed the cloth around his hips and dropped it to the floor. He eased off the bed and walked toward Bull, he slightly lifted onto his toes and raised his arms to drape them over Bull's broad shoulders. Bull's fingertips under his chin tilted his head back.

Bull's full beard had teased his chin and lips before the big man lowered his mouth to his. The kiss was slow and gentle, but he sensed the retrained need in Bull to take control—to be rougher. He loved what they'd done the night before, but he wanted the man to lose control. Bull was terrified of hurting him, doing something that triggered his panic. Except for the first night, he met Bull and the day Bull moved him in, he had never once been afraid of Bull.

As their lips brushed together and they played a game of chase and retreat, he sighed, "Are you holding back with me?"

"No, yes, maybe a little," Bull whispered in that sexy, gravelly tone of his.

When Bull was turned on or mad it got even deeper and rougher.

"Why? You promised never to touch me in anger, but I also know you and the guys have certain proclivities for rougher."

"Doesn't mean I want to be rough with you."

"Yes, you do."

"Is that what my boy wants?"

"You boy wants you not to hold back. I'm not breakable. And I'm definitely not broken, Bull."

"Never thought you were."

He believed Bull. Bull didn't see him lacking in any way. He dropped to his knees, dragging his hands down Bull's chest, and then wrapped them around Bull's cock. The thickness still surprised him. His hand barely able to circle it. He lifted it, held it against Bull's body and licked up the underside. Bull groaned and threaded his thick fingers in Gregory's hair.

He looked up to catch Bull' gaze as he flicked his tongue over the metal and traced the ring to where it disappeared into Bull's slit. He parted his lips and opened his mouth wide and took the fat head of Bull's dick into his mouth. Bull's tangy flavor burst on his tongue, and he moaned as he slowly started to bob along the length. He loved the contrast between unyielding metal and soft, silky skin teasing his tongue and palette.

"That's right, boy, you love sucking my cock, don't ya?"

His only answer a whimper. He gagged a bit with the ring touched the back of his throat and retreated. The coarse hairs on Bull's body added to his pleasure, his chest, hips, thighs, and ass. He loved Bull's hairiness.

He froze as Bull grabbed his head with both hands and held him still, Bull fucked his mouth in quick, shallow thrusts. Bull growled each time he gagged. The spit teasing the corners of his mouth and sliding down his chin embarrassed him, yet Bull never took his eyes off him.

Bull's cheeks were flushed, and his eyelids were heavy. He didn't know what came over him as he slid the fingers of his right hand between Bull's muscular ass and teased the tight, wrinkled skin of his hole.

"My boy wants to play."

He gave a short, small nod and pushed the tip of one finger inside.

"Fuck, baby," Bull rumbled, his stance widened.

He slowly worked the muscle but didn't thrust deep, just teased Bull as he moved quickly along Bull's length. The taste of Bull became stronger, and he retreated until he just sucked on the head, used his tongue to tug on the ring.

He was suddenly pulled to his feet by his hair. Bull's mouth slammed down onto his and Bull's tongue thrust deep and rough. Their groans mingled, and he followed Bull's lead as the man walked him backward toward the bed. His head swam, and he pushed his hips back as Bull slid his big, rough hands under the cotton of his pajama bottoms and pushed them down his hips.

A protest skipped and stalled on his tongue as he was turned and forced to bend over. He looked back over his shoulder to find Bull intensely staring down at his ass.

"Are you ready," Bull asked.

He opened his mouth to ask for what, but it ended in a yelp as Bull's left hand connected with one cheek, then the other. A gentle stroke soothed the burning skin of his ass. Spankings weren't something he'd ever considered erotic until that moment.

He whimpered and silently begged for more.

"Is that making my boy hard?" Bull asked, then Bull kicked his feet apart.

He tried to answer, but a rough hand pushed between his thighs and jacked his hard, aching dick. Each blow made him impossibly harder, and he'd come close to coming just from the spanking. Although the quick pumping of his cock made him dig his toes into the area rug he stood on.

Then it was gone.

The only thing left behind was the heat of his ass. He lowered his chin to his chest and took deep, even breaths. His cock hurt and leaked pre-come, the head angrily flushed.

"Why did you stop," he breathlessly asked.

"You were enjoying it too much. Stay where you are, don't move."

Instead of making some smart remark, he obeyed. He lifted his head to track Bull's every movement. To watch the play of muscle beneath his tanned skin. The flex of his ass. Bull moved as if he didn't have a care in the world. Bull opened the drawer, and just like the time before, he removed a condom and slick.

Bull closed it and laid down on the bed, scooted to the middle.

The big man removed the pillows from beneath his head and stretched out flat.

"You're going to crawl up here and straddle my head, I'm gonna eat that ass before I fuck it."

His thighs shook as he slowly crept up the bed, once he was at the head of the bed he did as Bull asked. Bull's hot breath fanned his hole. He couldn't believe he was doing it. His face flushed. Bull's hands cupped his ass and pulled apart his cheeks, he squeaked as Bull's tongue pushed against him.

"Hands on the fucking wall."

His palms flattened against the wall. He could feel the texture of brush strokes beneath the sensitive pads of his fingers and palms.

"Bull, please," he begged.

He didn't care how it made him sound, he wanted more. Without thought, he arched and rocked his hips, rode the probing tip of Bull's tongue. He threw his head back and whined to the ceiling as Bull's thumbs pulled at the sides of his hole, opened him further.

Bull groaned and rumbled against his skin. He put more of his weight on Bull's face as he rode Bull's tongue, felt the muscles give and let Bull fuck him deeper. Then

Bull's mouth disappeared and something broader and harder pushed inside.

He'd forgotten he'd left his dildo under the pillow. His cock began to soften. Fucking great, how em—every cognizant thought he had splintered as Bull's sucked his cock into his mouth and matched the rhythm with the shallow thrust of his toy. He dug his nails into the paint, and it gave slightly beneath the pressure.

His pace increased as he fucked into Bull's mouth and back onto the toy.

It was perfection and yet not enough. He jerked away, gently pulled the dildo from his ass and scooted down enough to wrap his hand around Bull. He didn't care how or when, but the man was already covered in latex. He held the man's dick as he pushed down passed the painful pop of the fat head.

He grabbed the bottle of slick with the other hand and squirted some in his palm, liberally coated Bull's dick on each upward and downward movement until the ride was smooth.

He fucked himself onto Bull in a quick, brutal pace until the room was filled with only the sounds of skin slapping against sweaty skin. Growls and moans blended, his was higher while Bull's dark and harsh. Bull's hands stroked up his chest and pinched at his small, pebbled nipples, he arched his back into Bull's touch.

He leaned forward as he lifted his hips and drove them back down, his cock slapping between his belly and Bull's hairy one. His mouth hovered over Bull's. They shared a kiss that was nothing but tongue and teeth—it held no finesse.

Sweat poured from his skin. Heat infused him from head to toe, the pleasure was pain. Bull's hands made their way to his ass, and his fingers dug into his parted crease, slick fingers pushed in on either side of Bull's cock.

His thighs and calves squeezed Bull's hips as his body arched and froze, Bull took over. Bull's hips lifted from the mattress, fucking his ass as hard and fast as possible as Bull pushed his fingers deeper with every thrust until he didn't think he could take more. The hard, metal of Bull's cock piercing tortured his prostate until his mouth fell open to scream, but nothing came out. The ecstasy rendering him silent.

Bull latched onto his bottom lip and held on tight as the man's movements faltered.

"Fuck, baby," Bull growled. "I'm not…"

He didn't need to hear anything else, he jerked off in time with Bull's thrusts. He slammed down onto Bull's cock and painted Bull's stomach with his cum. Bull splayed his hands on his lower back and ground their bodies together as Bull came. He sprawled on top of Bull and attempted to catch his breath. His muscles shook and twitched as he tried to get his brain working again.

His eyes closed tight as Bull slipped from him and let himself drift. He'd get up soon, not yet, but soon.

19 TRIAL BY FIRE

Bull lifted his left leg to place his ankle on his knee. He and Gregory were supposed to have a date, but Gregory got a call that a package of documents needed for the next day hadn't been delivered for the court date only a few days away.

"I'm so sorry about this."

Gregory apologized for the tenth time but didn't take his eyes off the screen. The shipping confirmation said the package made it to its destination, but the lawyer was saying it hadn't. Gregory couldn't exactly argue with the time sensitive situation.

It didn't bother him. He was just happy to get an evening with Gregory without a houseful of asshole brats. Even if that time was sitting in front of Gregory's desk while the man worked. It wasn't like Gregory hadn't sat on a barstool plenty since he'd moved in.

"Quit apologizing, if we don't make our reservation we'll pop into the diner for dinner. Stop stressing and just work."

He raised his hand to brace his elbow on the arm of his chair and rested his chin his palm and scratched his beard. It was the first time he'd come to work with Gregory, and he couldn't see the man sitting behind a desk. Gregory just seemed more comfortable curled up on the couch at home as he tapped away at his keyboard. He preferred when Gregory was home.

It wasn't any secret he knew Arnold had continued to make a nuisance of himself. He understood Gregory could take care of himself, but that didn't mean he had to like that his man was keeping secrets. He wouldn't deny he was a possessive bastard when it came to Gregory. His attempts to curb it failed. To be honest, he was waiting for the day Gregory got sick of him.

He scrubbed his hand over his face and repeated, try not to be an asshole, trying not to be an asshole. It had never worked, but it was worth a try.

"You want coffee," he asked.

He didn't want any but staring at Gregory, and all he wanted to do was spread the man out on Gregory's desk. Two weeks and he'd barely let Gregory out of their bed. And it was their bed. Gregory hadn't gone back to the guest room since the first night.

"Yes, please. Not as strong as you like though, please."

"Fine." He rolled his eyes. "Tea it is."

"Don't be an asshole."

He laughed as he stood and leaned across the desk to kiss Gregory's cute pout. Lingering wasn't an option, if he did, he would be where he'd tried to avoid. Gregory's sexy frame bent over. He'd forget dinner in a heartbeat.

He exited the office and made his way through the main room to the kitchenette in the back. The place was small, and he'd been there a few times. He pulled open cabinets until he found the coffee. He snarled his nose. The brand wasn't Gregory's favorite, but he doubted Gregory would drink more than a few sips.

He quickly started a pot brewing and leaned back against the counter to wait. He heard footsteps in the main room. Gregory had gone back and forth between the file room and his office a dozen times since they'd arrived. He might just take Gregory home and find something there, take-out was also an option. The coffee pot made its last gurgle, and he inhaled the rich scent of coffee, it wasn't as strong as he liked but what was he going to do?

With two mugs poured, one doctored with a ton of sugar and milk, he carried them back to Gregory. He entered just as the printer ceased and Gregory was gathering the papers.

"Here, drink this."

Gregory grabbed the bottom of the mug and brought it to his mouth.

"Thank you," Gregory sighed. "And it's not strong enough to strip paint. Aw, you're so sweet."

He playfully growled as Gregory set the papers aside and tweaked his beard.

"You need a trim." Gregory threw out the comment and went right back to work.

"The long, beard not working for you."

"You know I love it, so shut up."

"Someone's cranky."

Bull turned up his mug and took a few swallows as he tried not to laugh at what Gregory probably assumed was an intimidating look. It was too fucking cute.

"Someone needs to let me sleep."

"Quit looking so fucking sexy in my bed when I get home at night."

"I believe you told me that would be impossible."

"True. Your parents still leaving tomorrow?"

"Subtle subject change, Archer. Yes, I know how it'll pain you to see my mother go."

"I'm just thinking of her safety. Aggie is making herself a little too at home in Twitch's kitchen. She also let Pinkie loose, and it took us two days to find him."

"She said she was sorry."

"Yeah, but Twitch hates his routine fucked up and she cooked in his kitchen."

"I told her—"

"It's fine, just saying."

"You've been saying that a lot lately. I warned you, Bull."

"I know, I know, just finish work so we can get out of here...please."

"Fine."

He tried to repress a grin because Gregory was cute as fuck when he was all petulant and shit. He downed another swallow of his coffee and sat down. He leaned forward to place the mug on the edge of Gregory's desk.

Gregory had a point though, they needed more sleep, or at least he did. He'd waited so long to make Gregory's his maybe he needed to knock down his possessive tendencies a bit. Lifting his hands, he rubbed his suddenly tired eyes and then scrubbed his hands over his face.

His head felt too heavy, and it started to droop back. Gregory turned blurry like a mirage floating in the distance.

"Maybe we should just…" He frowned as his words slurred.

It was as if he were drunk, his limbs felt cumbersome, and his head floated above his shoulders. His tongue stuck to his palette. He attempted to reach for his coffee, his fingers were useless as he tried to pick up the cup.

"Greg…"

Gregory slumped over his keyboard. He pushed to his feet as he tried to call Gregory's name again. The world spun, he went down on his knees, but where pain should've exploded, there was nothing. His brain no longer worked and he could see the floor coming toward him as he collapsed. The last thing he remembered was his cheek meeting carpet.

■■■■

The stench of gasoline and heat hit him first, then his chest burned as he drew in another lungful of smoke. He tried to push up, but his body wasn't cooperating.

"If you don't get your fucking ass up, I'm going to fucking leave you here."

Hunter's voice caused him to open his eyes and pain exploded in his head. Worse than any hangover he had ever had. That's when everything registered, and he tried to go into fight mode, but his body just wouldn't listen. He rolled over to his back, and it seemed to take all the strength he had.

"What the fuck—"

"The ex is attempting to murder you." The words were broken by harsh hacking coughs.

"Gregory?"

"He's over there."

"Get him the fuck out."

"What about—"

"I don't give a fuck about me, get him out." He weakly pushed at Hunter's legs to get the man moving.

Thankfully, Hunter disappeared and reappeared seconds later with an unconscious Gregory limp in his arms.

"Go," he yelled.

"I'll come—"

"You won't do shit, stay with my man, go," he ordered.

His relief was short lived at Gregory being carried from the office. He laid there, panic quickly surfaced in his brain. Flames shimmered up the walls and danced along the ceiling, he glanced toward the open door. The scene was the same in the outer room. Smoke burned his eyes and tears flowed down his temples.

He reached for the edge of the desk and the overturned chair, he pulled only to fall back to the floor. The ceiling cracked, and beams creaked above him, he wasn't going to live if he didn't get moving and soon. He rolled back to his stomach, walking was out, so, he'd have to crawl. He used his hands to dig into the thick carpet.

Mere feet away seemed like miles. He hissed as a chunk of ceiling landed on his back. He jerked dislodging it, but he knew from the pain he hadn't moved quick enough to save himself from a burn. The sluggishness that infused his body only moments before disappeared in a rush of adrenaline. He struggled to his feet, his steps unsteady and he swayed as he raised his arms to try to protect his eyes from smoke and debris.

He was suddenly on his knees again. He'd remember the pain anywhere, someone took a bat or pipe to the backs of his knees.

"You couldn't fucking leave well enough alone, you had to take him. Brainwashed him."

Arnold. He darted a look over his shoulder and found the man tightly gripping an aluminum bat. Fucking moron, wood was the way to go if you wanted maximum damage.

"You beat him. Fucking locked him in a closet. You didn't—"

Lightweight or not, air whooshed from his already singed lungs as the metal landed sharply on his side. Agony moved through him and knew he had a least a few cracked ribs, badly bruised if he were lucky. He wasn't that fucking lucky.

"All he had to do was listen. Now, you've ruined my plan again. He was supposed to die. If I can't—"

"You gonna die in here too."

"No, I just wanted to make sure you were gone. Then I can get my husband to come home. Killing you will be even better than I planned."

"Fuck you—"

He focused, the momentum of the bat slowed, and he lifted his arm to block the first shot. Bones broke, and he hollered through clenched teeth. He cradled his arm against his chest, and as he tried to block the next blow, he didn't make it in time. It landed on the side of his head. The echo of metal meeting bone, the hiss of flame, and the creaking of wood joined together. His head swam, and wetness trickled down and tickled the shell of his ear.

"Don't worry, I'll take good care of him."

He made a fruitless attempt to grab Arnold with his good hand but missed when the man stepped back. Arnold disappeared in a break between flames. He couldn't leave Gregory. He loved him. Arnold would break the man Bull came to love. He'd crawl from the fucking building. He didn't give a fuck what it took.

"Bull," Hunter called out.

"I told you to fucking stay—"

"Gregory frightens me more than you. Get the fuck up."

Hunter hauled him too quickly to his feet, and the world dimmed, became nothing more than flame and ash before the words faded.

20 GREGORY WASN'T GIVING UP ON BULL

Psycho was in jail…again. Arnold had run into Psycho as he had tried to escape through the back exit. Hunter had tried to say he wasn't going back in for Bull. That wasn't happening. He wouldn't live without Bull. Hunter had tried some bullshit that Bull ordered him not to come back for Bull. Bull might think he was in charge but Gregory was, and Hunter wasn't going to disobey him.

Both Hunter and Psycho went back in for Bull but took different routes. He couldn't believe Arnold tried to kill them. Yes, the man seemed unhinged and a huge bastard, but a murderer, Gregory wouldn't have assumed that.

He dipped the rag back into the warm water and rung it out, then went back to gently cleaning Bull's face, well, what he could see of it anyway. A bandage covered his entire head and Bull's left eye. They'd cleaned him before surgery to relieve the pressure on his brain, but some soot still remained in Bull's thick beard. As he'd done countless times over the last three days, he had cataloged each bruise and cut, every burn.

They'd braced Bull's left forearm to wait for the swelling to go down before they cast it. The fracture wasn't bad and hadn't required surgery. He dropped the cloth into the plastic basin and set it aside.

He was so angry with Bull. Bull ordered Hunter to leave Bull behind, to get him out, and to not come back for him. It was chivalrous but dumb as hell. He traced the skin on Bull's chest, avoided the bandages wrapped around his abdomen. Badly bruised ribs. He wanted his man back; wanted Bull to open his eyes so he could see the mismatched colors and know Bull was okay.

He refused to cry anymore. The first two days he was there, that's all he did. Bull needed him to be strong.

The door opened behind him. Crave and Tank were posted outside, so, he didn't worry about who was coming in. He glanced over his shoulder to find Scary. Scary acted as a messenger.

"News," Scary asked.

"No, same as yesterday. What about Arnold?"

Scary walked to stand on the opposite side of the bed.

Gregory took Bull's hand, turned it over and gently traced the thick callouses on his fingertips and palm.

"Peaches is on it. He's trying some bullshit about it being accidental. Thorpe is being Thorpe."

Sheriff Thorpe was a bigot and hated the Twirled and Brawlers Crews with an all-consuming rage.

"Peaches won't let that stand."

"No, she won't. Well, Elijah and I picked up Twitch on our way here. He's upset, I just wanted to warn you."

"Mom and Dad?"

"They're in the waiting room just like yesterday and the day before. Aggie wants to rush in, but your dad is keeping her away until you're ready."

"I just can't—"

"No need to explain. We've been through this time or two. Priest's ex tried to kill Lucky in a hit and run, we knew to give Priest space with his man. This is your place, we're just here for backup."

"Like the guards outside?"

A small smile tugged at the corner of Scary's mouth. "We got no faith in Thorpe keeping Arnold locked up. We called in a few favors."

"And," he asked.

"He's in deep with a dealer Peaches defended a time or two. He lost his job about a year ago."

"So, he's..."

"Been going through his retirement and savings like crazy keeping up with appearances. He's about six months from losing the house."

"The fire wasn't about getting me back?"

"It probably was, fucker wanted a meal ticket. You definitely fucked shit up when you left."

"Was rescued."

"You should've come to us with this shit. You're Landon's friend."

"I was—"

"Embarrassed, yeah, we get that, and you didn't really know us. Don't make that fucking mistake again."

"I won't. Could you give me a bit longer with Bull before you bring Twitch in? Our youngest—"

Scary's laugh gruff and the man shook his head.

"I've heard the stories about you. You adopt. Just like Elijah and Landon. Each crew has a Papa Bear."

"Bull's more the bear type."

"True, but Mama Bear sounds weird. We called in Lucky and Priest to keep Twitch balanced for a bit so just let us know when you're ready."

"Thanks."

"No thanks among friends or family and you're both."

Scary left without another word.

He brought his full attention back to Bull. He felt the smile pulling at his mouth even in sleep his brow still bore deep furrows. He loved his grumpy man. Bull needed to wake up so he could tell him. The regret he kept that from Bull would eat him alive.

"Come on, baby, you have to wake up. How am I going to raise our kids alone?"

The heart monitor kicked up a notch.

"Oh, don't like that, huh?"

"You don't get out of my way, you'll be thankful you're in the hospital."

Polly's enraged voice caused him to flinch.

"Honey, you need to—"

"I don't need to do shit, you even touch me, and I'll break every finger that brushes against me. Archer taught me how, think about that."

He didn't know if Polly was threatening Crave, Psycho, or Hal. It didn't matter because he didn't doubt she'd follow through.

Seconds later, the door opened, and a pale and pissed off Polly barged in.

"Do you know how many people I've threatened to kill in the last twenty-four hours. I went toe to toe with a General to get in contact with Hank."

"Hello, Polly."

"Why the hell is he still asleep? Lazy bastard."

The anger in her voice at odds with the tender way she took Bull's other hand.

"I thought you'd be here sooner."

"Don't start. I won't put up with two of you. Archer is enough."

"Did you make Hal stay in the hall?"

"Yes, he's hovering. My husband knows I hate that. Any change?"

He was beginning to hate that question, he'd lost count of how many times he had heard it.

"No, I was just telling him he couldn't leave me to raise our kids alone."

The even beat changed again, and he couldn't help smiling.

"I don't think he likes I'm adopting the crew."

"Why not? It isn't like he hadn't already done it. He loves those boys as much as he does Hank. He might bitch and moan about it, but he wouldn't know what to do without them."

"I want him to wake up so I can yell at him for being an idiot. He told Hunter to leave him."

"And you made sure that didn't happen. I'll be forever grateful for that."

He observed the loving expression on Polly's face as she stared down at Bull. At that moment, he understood why Bull loved his ex-wife so much. They hadn't been able to make their romantic relationship work, but the friendship between the former spouses was stronger than any he'd ever seen.

"Bull was destined to be my best friend, Gregory. He wasn't perfect, and his drinking turned our marriage into hell sometimes, but not once did I ever want to give him up.

"I knew he was gay before he told me, but I was selfish." She glanced at him with watery eyes.

"Selfish?" he asked.

"I lived for his smiles. They didn't happen a lot, but when they did," she sighed. "His entire face lit up, and he was so handsome, and he was the boy I grew up with. And when he'd come home from work, and he'd dance me around the kitchen. Archer was my best friend again. I held all those memories close when the dark and angry man appeared. I could've—"

"Polly, holding the what-ifs close isn't worth overshadowing those good times. It happened when it was supposed to, and I'm just as selfish. If he'd come out sooner, then he wouldn't be mine."

"Gregory, Archer was as destined to be yours as he was mine."

"If this sappy shit keeps going on I'm going—"

He and Polly jumped up at the same time as Bull's deep growl broke into their conversation. They threw their arms around him, squeezed the air out of him, and they kissed his cheeks.

"You do this shit to us again, and we'll kill you," they shouted in unison.

"How long have I been out, because you two have gotten a bit too close."

"Shut up," they did it again.

"Water."

He left Polly to cuddle Bull and filled a plastic cup with water, then stuck a straw in it.

"Sip only."

"I'm a grown ass fucking—"

He shoved the straw into his mouth to shut him up. Awake minutes and he was already an ass.

"Don't be an asshole, Archer."

"I'll go let everyone know he's awake and then find the doctor."

"Thanks, Polly."

Polly rolled her eyes, brushed a kiss against his cheek, and then straightened. Before she headed for the door, she gave Bull one last, long look. He'd forever be grateful to Polly for taking care of Bull.

Bull's head fell back, and he set the cup on the bedside table.

"Don't you ever fucking do that to me again, Archer."

"You were more important than me."

"If you weren't wounded and in the hospital, I would so smack you right now."

"Violence, I ask again, how long have I been out?"

He studied Bull's pale, drawn face and then leaned forward to press a quick kiss to Bull's dry lips.

"Today is day three."

"I don't remember much."

"Arnold took a bat to your skull."

"Why is my eye covered?"

"It's fine, part of the ceiling collapsed just Hunter was getting you out. You got one helluva cut to your eyelid. Your eye is scratched but should be fine in a week or so. You probably get to wear a sexy patch.

"You really can't do that to me, Archer, I stood outside helpless, and it seemed like hours before I saw Hunter carrying you out."

"What about Arnold?"

"He tried to escape out the back door. He ran into a wall named Psycho."

"Is Psycho in jail?"

"Yep, but Peaches is on it, so, I don't see him spending much more time there."

"So, he's not dead."

"Arnold probably wishes he was. He spent two days in a room down the hall. Psycho broke every bone in both Arnold's hands."

"I love you."

He blinked several times as he stared at Bull. Did he hear that right?

"What?"

"I was going to tell you when we got home. I fucked this up, didn't I?"

"No."

"But you're not—"

He slammed his mouth against Bull's and didn't stop until he flinched at the pain-filled groan against his lips.

"Sorry, sorry."

It wasn't the most romantic announcement of love, but, hell, if he wanted sweet he wouldn't have fallen for Bull. He loved every gruff, cranky inch of the man.

"You're not saying it, I did—"

"I love you too, don't think I don't. You get a do-over when I get you home. You can be all romantic, flowers and all, but right now, it was perfect."

"You're fucking weird."

"Did you think someone normal would love you?"

"You got a fucking point."

He covered Bull's face in gentle kisses as the room filled with both crews. This was his family, and he wouldn't regret it. No matter how bad the last few years were, it brought him to Bull and the crews. He'd take the bad because this was beyond anything he'd ever dreamed and it was only the beginning.

EPILOGUE: BULL WAS TOO OLD FOR THIS SHIT

Six months passed, Arnold was in jail and finally out of their lives. Bull watched as Gregory fussed over Hunter's tie. Hunter's cheeks were bright pink as Gregory fawned over him. Since Arnold's attempt to kill them, Hunter became the victim of Gregory's fatherly attentions. He didn't think Hunter had much affection when he'd grown up and was still uncomfortable with it, but that didn't stop Gregory.

Polly, Hal, and Hank stood off to the side with Landon and Elijah. Bernie and Stacey spoke softly as Bernie cradled Stacey on her lap.

His yard was filled with his people. He hadn't realized how alone he was until his group grew larger over the past decade.

He shook his head as he turned his head to watch Juvie and Princess chase a squealing Matty around the yard. Psycho was in one of the rocking chairs with two tiny bundles cradled in his arms. The big man growled at anyone who tried to take them. Gunner and Hendrix aka Rage nicknamed because the baby was always pissed off. He already had the Psycho glare down at only a few months. It didn't look good for the future.

Gregory adored Rage and was the only person other than Psycho who could hold the kid without Rage having a complete meltdown. Gregory bounced up onto the porch, and Psycho turned his body away from Gregory.

He knew what was about to happen.

"Give him to me," Gregory demanded.

"You had him for an hour, dammit, he's mine."

"You got two, share, bastard," Gregory yelled.

"Fine, but if he cries I get him—"

Gregory plucked the tiny baby from Psycho's arms, and Rage actually giggled as Gregory cooed at him. They'd already talked about no kids for them. He was too old for that shit.

He tugged at the collar of his dress shirt.

"Let's get this show on the road, people," Lily yelled.

Lily wore a long flowing dress of white linen. He recognized Lucky's work. He still couldn't get over Lucky's skills. If people looked at the man, they wouldn't think he screamed seamstress.

He was dragged to the top of the porch steps, and Gregory bounced over to stand beside him.

"No," Gregory feigned right when Psycho attempted to take Rage back. "Mine."

"Mine."

"Children, he's a baby, not a damn toy!"

"Mine," Gregory muttered ignoring Lily.

Ben hauled Psycho away as Ben soothed the bigger man's feelings.

174

Gregory stood in front of him, Rage cradled in his arms, and Gregory stared up at him. He still couldn't believe Gregory was his. Ten years ago, he'd given up on finding this. He glanced around the yard. His crew and the Twirled one filled the area at the bottom of the steps. His life was only described as lonely until he walked into Brawlers for a job. He'd adopted a bunch of grown ass kids and found lifelong friendships.

To top all of it off, he was about to marry his man surrounded by their family.

Lily reached out and took their hands.

"Today we gather to join Gregory and Bull in front of their family, chosen by love…"

His gaze caught Gregory's and realized he'd gone through hell just for this moment—for this man. He had to have done something right, he didn't know when, but it happened, and that's all that mattered. He'd had a lot of Day Ones over the years, but today, today was a Day One he'd embrace for a lifetime.

THE END

ABOUT THE AUTHOR

By day, J.M. is an introverted cook hiding out in her kitchen in the middle of nowhere Ohio, by night and any free time she may have, she is a writer of mainly LGBTQ Fiction and Erotica. Although. she's equal opportunity when it comes to telling a story, she'll even write a bit of straight erotic romance when the mood strikes.

She has been writing for years in old notebooks. At the age of eight, she wrote the worst poem in the history of poetry, but it sparked her love for writing. She reads too much and loves to get lost in other worlds and her favorite stories have to include laughter and having the reader doing at least one double take. Thirty-something, forever restless she uses her stories to ground herself, and find her place of peace.

WHERE TO FIND J.M.
www.jmdabneyauthor.com